Late Summer Break

Ann B. Knox

Also by Ann B. Knox

Stonecrop

Late Summer Break

Ann B. Knox

Papier-Mache Press
Watsonville, CA

04 03 02 01 00 99 98 97 96 95   10 9 8 7 6 5 4 3 2 1

ISBN: 0-918949-64-5 Softcover
ISBN: 0-918949-65-3 Hardcover

Cover art by Annie Aird
Cover and interior design by Cynthia Heier
Copyediting by Shirley Coe
Composition by Leslie Austin
Manufactured by Malloy Lithographing, Inc.

Grateful acknowledgment is made to the following publications which first published some of the material in this book:
Warren Wilson Review for "Passing on Messages"; *Zuzu'z Petals* for "Another Mountain; *Over-the-Wall* for "Survivors"; *Metropolitan* for "Marsh Island"; *New Letters* (Winner of New Letters Literary Award) for "Magnus Isn't Here"; *The MacGuffin* for "Etcetera Period"; *Phoebe* for "Late Summer Break"; *The MacGuffin* for "Floyd"; *Antietam Review* for "Domain"; *Green's Magazine* for "Coin"; and *Intro* for "A Way Out for the Spirit."

Library of Congress Cataloging-in-Publication Data

Knox, Ann. B., 1926-
    Late summer break / Ann Knox.
       p. cm.
    ISBN 0-918949-65-3 (hardcover : acid-free paper) : $14.00. —
    ISBN 0-918949-64-5 (softcover : acid-free paper) : $9.00
    1. Middle aged persons—United States—Social life and customs—
Fiction.   I. Title.
PS3561.N6857L38 1995
813'.54—dc20   94-41553
                                          CIP

For my children:
Ron, Ann, Marion, Gordon, Joanna, Andrew

Acknowledgments

I am grateful to the Pennsylvania Council on the Arts
for fellowships which helped support me while writing some
of these stories, and to the Virginia Center for the Creative
Arts for unbroken time to work in a quiet place
during several residencies.

Contents

Late Summer Break

Ann B. Knox

Marsh Island

Hallie drove past the low, white milking barn then slowed to turn onto a narrow causeway leading across the marsh to the island. The crunch of her tires on the clamshell surface brought a familiar lift of expectation; she leaned forward as the road curved into the trees. Without leaves, the woods were brighter than she remembered, and when she broke into the clearing, she caught a glimpse of marsh beyond. The landscape was defined by tones of grey—the winter field, a house with weathered shingles, bare woods. A red station wagon parked by the steps jarred the monochromatic scene.

It was Len's car, her daughter's. Hallie had hoped to be there first; she'd intended to have the groceries put away and the house aired before Len arrived. As she lifted her suitcase from the car, she caught the smell of pine smoke.

"Ma." Len crossed the millstone terrace in wide strides to welcome her mother.

Hallie, startled by her own delight at Len's hug, had forgotten her daughter was taller than she.

"Here, let me take that." Len picked up the suitcase.

"I'll fetch the groceries from the trunk," Hallie said.

"I've already put some in."

"When did you get here?"

"Last night. I wanted to warm the house before you came."

"Last night?" Hallie lifted the brown sacks from the car and carried them into the kitchen. "You've got it nice and warm. Was there enough wood?"

"Phil and I came out with the boys for a weekend, and Richie brought us a load in his pickup. The boys helped stack it."

"Trust Richie."

"You're in Gran's room. The fire's going."

1

Len would have taken the big room then, the one Hallie's parents added after she and Mark were married. It looked over the marshes with windows on three sides and sun all day. Hallie always stayed there unless Len and the children were visiting at the same time, then she slept on the pullout bed in the den.

"A fire so early?"

"The room was damp, besides it's cheerful."

Len set her mother's suitcase on the bed covered with a blue-and-white Indian spread.

"You've changed the spread."

"I picked it up at a sale. I never liked the one Gran had. The circles looked like angry faces."

It had been an old candlewick with a ring pattern in blue and white. Hallie hadn't liked it either.

"She always used it."

"It's our place now; we can change things."

Yes, they could change things. Her mother had died three months ago. She had left the island with its summer house and a small legacy to both of them: "the two remaining Helens," she wrote in a letter attached to her will. Hallie had always assumed the place would be hers.

Ever since Hallie was born, they had spent summers there. Her first memory was of her father carrying a horse-shoe crab from the creek. He'd showed her the lidless eyes and strange flippered feet; when he set it on its back, the crab had bent in half and tried to right itself using its spike tail. She knew every foot of the island and the farm on the mainland as well. Her grandparents had sold the farmland to Richie's father who had built the milking barn for his Holstein herd, and now, like his father, Richie kept an eye on the island in winter when no one lived there.

"I like the spread," Hallie said. "It's the same color."

Len stood by the window looking out; she spoke without turning. "It's lovely here in winter. Why did Gran use it only in summer?"

"The island was only part of her life. Too far from New York. Besides, the pipes had to be drained."

"Richie showed Phil how. It's not hard to drain the pipes."

"It was a summer place."

"Dad loved it."

"Yes, he loved it."

The year Hallie met Mark, she'd invited him to the island. She had planned long walks on the marshes and sailing on the river, but Mark and her father had spent the time building a tool shed. They had both served with the air force in Europe, her father as a colonel, Mark as a corporal, and they took to each other right away. After four years' absence, her father had reclaimed the place by building on it.

Hallie had carried out cold drinks and watched the two men work. They'd nail a line of shingles, pause to talk, then pick up where they'd left off. She felt as if she were interrupting, and instead of walks with Mark, she and her mother had picked blackberries and made preserves. Her mother talked about her early married years, and Hallie felt an ease with her she had not known before. By the end of the summer, she and Mark were engaged, the shed was finished, and the kitchen window gleamed with rows of dark red jelly.

Len was peeling potatoes when Hallie came into the kitchen. It was brightly lit and seemed somehow tidier than last summer. "It looks different," Hallie said.

"I weeded out the spices. Some were ten years old—cinnamon sticks marked twenty-five cents."

Hallie had done that one year when Len was little: her mother never noticed, or never spoke of it. Her mother rarely let Hallie know if she were angry or upset; Hallie had to watch and guess.

"Do you want tea before we start?" Len asked.

"I think I'll go for a walk. I want to say hello to the island again."

Len looked up from the potato she was peeling. "Another reason I came early was that I'd never stayed here alone. I wanted to know what it felt like." She glanced at Hallie. "Besides, I was glad for a break from the boys."

Hallie shook out a jacket and stepped into the Wellingtons she kept in the closet. She wondered if Len had had to learn to read her face as she had her mother's. Was she as closed as her mother had been?

It was cold outside, raw and windy; patches of snow lay in the woods and on the north slope of the hill. She crossed the grey lawn to where it met the marsh; here the grass changed texture and the strandline, a band of seaweed and flotsam, marked the winter's high tides. Across the marshes, a ridge of bare hills dropped to a stretch of pewter sea.

She turned along the island's perimeter. As a girl, she had circled it daily looking for treasures, collecting round cork floats the fishermen used on their nets. A generation before, her mother had found glass balls knotted in string, then Len brought home bright Styrofoam floats that seemed brash beside the older weathered trophies.

Hallie had not been on the island since she visited her mother last summer, and this was her first chance to claim her inheritance. Hers and Len's. She closed her eyes for a second. Why did her mother do it that way? It wasn't that Hallie wouldn't welcome Len and Phil and the boys. She knew Len felt as she did about the place, but she had expected to choose the bedspreads and see to the wood herself.

Cold pressed through the soles of her boots, and her toes felt numb. She watched her footing; her balance was no longer as steady as it used to be. If Len hadn't been there, she would have taken the driftwood cane her mother always used.

In the past decade, a new species of reed, tall as pampas grass, had begun to invade the marsh, growing along the border between woods and wetlands. It had brought back the muskrats. Last summer, her mother found a trap on a narrow path trampled through the reeds. Someone had run a trap line, Richie had told her. Phil posted the island, tacking yellow signs on the trees. "Won't do no good," Richie said. "In winter when no one's here, they come acrost the marsh anyway."

The reeds pushed her path out from the shoreline, and she missed seeing the granite boulder that had been her sitting place as a girl. Behind the reeds, the east meadow rose to an edge of trees where sumacs had begun to close its borders. She should get Richie to take the brush cutter over the field before the woods reclaimed it. It was there on the top of the meadow that she and Mark had thought of building a house for themselves, but he had died before he was ready to retire.

Wind picked up on the north side, and when she reached the causeway, she took the short way back along the road rather than finish circling the island. In the woods, a Christmas fern flattened by winter showed no sign yet of new growth. Trees creaked in the wind, and, for an instant, she thought she heard a faint whine. She stood still to listen, but it was only the high hum in her head that never left her in complete silence.

When she got back to the house, the living room fire was burning, and Len had set the table.

"Drink?"

"I'll have wine." Hallie leaned back in the morris chair with her feet on the fire bench. It was her mother's chair. Len poured wine for both of them and lifted her glass.

"To Gran."

"To Ma."

Len sat opposite Hallie, her feet on the other end of the bench. She had called a few weeks ago and suggested they meet on the island to "get things in order."

"Phil and I love the island," Len said. "We could do some work on the house." Hallie watched her daughter's face. "It's only an hour from our place. I'd like to spend summers here the way we used to. Let the boys range the marshes. We even thought of winterizing the house."

Hallie turned to look at the fire. She had imagined herself on the island and that Len and the boys would visit. She'd seldom had the place to herself. Once during college, she'd come for spring break to work on a paper, and a late snowstorm had cut her off for three astounding days. She had, of course, been there alone with the children and a couple of times with Mark, but never long enough.

"Gran let things go a bit," Len said.

"Like the spread?" Hallie glanced around the room. "I guess we could do with a new rug. This is pretty shabby."

"We thought of tile."

"Tile?"

"There's no upkeep; it's easy to clean."

"I don't know. I like the wood floor and the bright rag rugs." Hallie nodded to the row of fox hunting prints over the mantle. "We could get rid of those."

"Gran said a grateful patient gave them to Grandpa."

"Why don't you take them?" Hallie wondered where Len would hang them; her house was spare and white, surprisingly neat with their two boys. But tastes shift. Hallie herself had fancied the Scandinavian look when she first married, but her mother-in-law sent her a van load of Victorian furni-

5

ture. She eventually grew fond of it.

"I don't want to change things much," Len said. She twisted her glass as she spoke. "This was Gran's place. She told me her mother gave it to her as a wedding present before they sold the farm."

"Yes, it was her island." The fire popped, and a spark fell onto the hearth. Hallie leaned forward to brush it back. "The east field needs cutting," she said. "It used to be pasture, but trees are moving in fast."

"You've always liked that spot."

"It has the prettiest view on the island. Your father and I talked of building a house there once."

"Your own place? Did you ask Gran?"

Hallie shook her head without turning from the fire. "You know, I never dared. I was afraid she might say no."

"You could now."

"I could."

Len got up and came back with cheese and crackers. "I had a call from the lawyer. He needs the deed to the house. Do you know where it is?"

"In the panel drawer," Hallie said.

Len looked up. "What drawer?"

"In the bookcase."

"There's a drawer?"

Hallie was pleased Len didn't know. Her mother had shown her the hiding place when she was ten, and she had never told anyone, not even her brothers. She liked sharing a secret with her mother. A few times, she had looked inside, but there was only a single sealed envelope.

Hallie started to get up, but sat back. "You'll need a chair to get it," she said. "On the top shelf over the *Everyman* edition. Put your hand under the molding; it comes out."

Len reached up and pulled out the narrow drawer; she stepped down and set it on the bench in front of her mother. "How come I never knew?"

"It was a secret." Hallie lifted up the long envelope, slightly yellowed. On it, *Deed* was written in her mother's old-fashioned script. The glue had dried, and she was able to open it without a knife. The paper, embossed with a notary's seal, was made out in three names: her mother's, Hallie's, and Len's maiden name. It was dated 1948.

"The year I was born."

Hallie looked at Len. "It's been ours all along."

"Why didn't she tell us?" Len said.

"Gran liked secrets. They gave her power." As Hallie said it, she knew it was true.

"I don't. I don't like being left out," Len said.

"Neither do I."

Len picked up the document and turned the pages over. "But I'm glad she didn't tell us; I would have wanted to lay claim. It would have been hard on Gran, us intruding."

Hallie felt a sting at her words. How did Len know so easily what had taken her years to recognize? Hallie had known the island would be hers and had resented having to wait. She despised herself for thinking this and rarely admitted to the feeling. Had her mother passed on her penchant for keeping secrets, even from herself?

For her mother's funeral, Hallie had sent out the announcements and arranged the service and refreshments afterward. And she had liked doing it. As she greeted her mother's friends, she was aware of a shift in how she spoke, how she felt. Her mother no longer buffered her from entering old age. She was old now, and Len, middle-aged. Had the cycle come round? Did Len feel the same untidy tugs with her that she had with her mother? In the last few years, she had spent more time with her mother and had come to accept her secrets, her reticence. Hallie didn't see Len often enough; maybe now that would change.

By the end of dinner, the fire had burned down. Len went out for more logs. Hallie could see a square of sky with a few stars through the open door. As Len came in, arms full, she paused in the doorway.

"What is it?"

"I don't know. A dog, I guess. A yap." She kicked the door shut behind her.

"I thought I heard something when I came through the woods earlier."

Len set the logs in the wood bin and put one on the fire. She walked back to the door and opened it again.

"Come here a minute, Ma."

Hallie pushed herself up to stand in the doorway beside Len. The air was cold and the stars brighter than she ex-

7

pected. A distinct bark came from the edge of the island, then a whine.

"Something's caught. Remember the trap? I bet something's caught in the trap."

They looked at each other. "We'd better go."

Hallie fetched the big spotlight from the closet and a pocket light for Len. They pulled on boots and parkas, and as they went out the door, Hallie picked up her mother's driftwood stick.

"It's at the north end."

They walked down the path that led to the marsh and turned along the drift line. Where the reeds began, they stopped to listen.

"Further on." They walked another hundred yards and stopped again.

"Turn out the light," Hallie said. "We might frighten it."

There was no moon, but the reeds rose in a pale wall beside them, and the marsh stretched into darkness. Half a mile away on the Neck, the headlights of a car moved along the road, and a halo from Richie's barn backlit the island. Winter silence held; the reeds rattled lightly; then again, the low rasp. They moved on, Hallie using her stick for balance. Suddenly, Len stopped and held up her hand. A low growl came from inside the reeds close to them, a sudden half bark, half howl. Hallie turned on the spotlight. It's beam picked out a pair of amber eyes, a small triangular face, and the gleam of teeth.

"Oh god, a fox."

"It's caught," Len said.

"We have to free it."

Len unzipped her parka and took it off.

"Careful, it might be rabid," Hallie said.

Len held the coat wide in front of her and moved in. The animal coiled back, it's mouth in a fierce smile. Len threw the jacket, then squatted to collect it, but the fox writhed away and snapped at her hand. She pulled back.

"Damn," Len said.

Hallie slid off her coat. "Here, use both." She moved closer, beaming the spotlight on the fox. It pulled back, and the rusted chain tethered to a pipe clacked taut; its foreleg, held by steel teeth, precise and oddly tidy, stretched toward them as if in greeting.

Len leaned over the fox, dropped the two jackets, and moved in fast, gathering the jackets around the struggling animal. The paw with the trap attached extended from the bundle.

"Can you get it open?"

Hallie set down the light and squatted to pry open the metal jaws. She felt the fur and the rough pad of the fox's paw. Her fingers could not force the trap open.

Len got a fresh hold on the wrapped animal. "Here, take it. I'll try. Hold on tight." Len lifted the awkward bundle.

Hallie put her hands around it and pulled it close under her arm. The fox gave a short cry. "Hey fella, easy there." She could feel it struggle, pressing its hind paws against her belly.

Len held the flashlight in her mouth, and with two hands, worked to open the trap. Suddenly the trap clicked and dropped on the ground. Hallie felt the animal stiffen. Len turned her light on the paw. A flash of bone showed through torn skin, but little blood.

"What do you think?" Hallie said.

"It's probably broken."

"Animals heal."

"He's been licking it."

"Shall we let him go?"

"Yes," Len said. "Let him go."

Hallie set the bundle down, stood back quickly, and lifted the jackets with her stick. The fox pulled loose, its damp fur slicked close to its sides.

"It's a vixen," Hallie said.

All three of them stood a moment breathing hard. Then the fox shook her whole body, raising the fur, and, as if to orient herself, looked left and right before she slipped into the reeds.

"Good luck, little fox," Hallie said.

"Damn them."

"What can we do?"

"They'll keep coming across the marsh, as Richie says, so long as no one lives here."

Hallie looked toward Len. She could not see her face, only her profile against the night sky. "It's our island," Hallie said. "We have to claim it."

Len was quiet for a bit. "Our island," she said. "I like that."

Hallie planted her stick in the soft ground. She looked past the reeds to the dim bulk of hill where her house would lie just below the crest.

A Way Out for the Spirit

A sign for the sale, tacked on a telephone pole, pointed up a dirt road that ran toward the ridge. It would be one of the small homesteads settled on the poor land against the steep side of the valley. Carrie felt a vague excitement that reminded her of going to the county fair as a girl, the feeling that she might win a prize that would change everything. But all she wanted was a few mixing bowls and a crock to fill the shelves her husband, John, had put up for her in their cabin.

It was sad to see the old people squeezed from their land by the high cost of farming, loans they couldn't pay off, or taxes. Sometimes they held onto an acre or two and put up one of those modular houses that appeared efficient and complete. Once after she and John missed a few weekends at the cabin, they came back to find a new house in the middle of what had been an empty meadow.

This was a perfect autumn day. Heavy rain had passed through in the night and then a cold front; the sun had risen with mist streaming up the ridges. The road ran through open farmland—fields of alfalfa, green and ready for a last cutting, and stands of corn turning brown—and in the distance, mountains hard-edged, blue. She wished John was with her, but he rarely came to sales. He said he needed to varnish the shelves so they would be ready to use by Sunday, and he had to replace the overflow pipe from the spring.

The farm up for sale was set in a narrow dip, barn on one side of the road, house on the other. It was an old log building; the squared-off timbers showed at one corner where the siding was torn. Outbuildings of board and batten had weathered to silver grey. The pasture, now empty of livestock, served for parking. Carrie was reluctant to drive onto the cropped greensward and leave tire marks, but cars and trucks were already lined in uneven rows. They were mostly farm trucks with tools or straw in the bed; some had yellow lights across the top or gun racks on the rear window; a couple were vintage models John would have appreciated. Then there was a scatter of big, comfortable cars farm women like to drive, with only a few small foreign cars like hers.

She pulled up next to a green van with D.C. plates. Probably an antique dealer from the city. They were always at the sales, cool, knowing, ready to skim off family treasures, polish the history out of them, and sell them in the understated elegance of their Georgetown shops.

Carrie walked toward the house. The place had an odd troubled air; people milled about or congregated in clusters with an occasional stir of sudden activity as at a wedding or an accident. She stopped by a table set in front of the house to sign the auctioneer's book. The woman smiled as she handed Carrie a bidding number. They recognized each other from the A & P where the woman worked at the checkout counter.

The sale was already underway. From behind the barn came the rise and fall of the auctioneer's ritual chant as he offered the farm machinery. This gave Carrie time to walk the rows of goods for sale. The house had been eviscerated. Its contents were spread out on sawbuck tables, lined on the lawn, and hung over the porch rails—small private articles exposed to sun and air perhaps for the first time in years: combs, soap dishes, a hand mirror. They were touched and turned by strangers. Carrie could guess the family's size and fortunes by the kitchen ware: bits of depression glass given as bonuses with soap powder in the '30s, brown earthenware mixing bowls that would hold enough dough for six loaves, Pyrex and Tupperware dishes, an iron skillet the size of a manhole cover, but only a small skillet gleamed with the patina of recent use.

Under the maple, the church auxiliary had a food table with a coffee urn and big pots of chili. Two women folded hot dogs into soft buns, setting them on paper plates next to jars of relish. Other women chatted among themselves drinking coffee or sodas while the farm tools were being auctioned. They treated each other with the offhand ease of long-standing acquaintance. A bunch of little kids swung round the house and ran out toward the barn. On the porch, two girls played with their dolls under an overturned wicker chair. A red-haired boy carrying a can of Coke leaned down and spoke to them, then handed the soda to an old woman who moved back and forth in a straight-backed rocker.

Carrie watched a young couple looking at furniture set in rows on the grass. They stopped to inspect an overstuffed armchair from the fifties; they poked the seat, touched the upholstery, uncertain what to look for. A small boy squatted beside an elegant piano stool with a screw seat and metal feet in the shape of eagles' claws holding a glass ball. He spun the seat with his hand, then sat himself on the stool and swung around until a man told him to get off.

A dozen or so quilts had been draped over the porch rails: some were crazy quilts made with patches of coarse linsey-woolsey, blankets, and corduroy; others were finely worked in calico. Under the corner of a Wedding Ring spread, Carrie saw an edge of rough woven wool. She pulled the quilt aside; it was a Navaho rug. She stood absolutely still; she knew with her whole body, the piece was superb— Two Grey Hills pattern, fine workmanship, and all natural wool colors except the red which might be a piece of Spanish bayeta. She could tell it was old, very old by the quality of spinning, the twist of wool, the irregular borders, and a tell-tale white thread that ran from the inside grey diamond across the border to the edge. A way out for the spirit.

With her back to the crowd, Carrie squatted to inspect the weave. She felt a seed embedded in the wool. It had been growing a century, possibly two centuries ago on a dry mesa. She leaned to smell the lanolin oil. John had taught her about these rugs. He told her with loving detail as he showed her the ones in his father's house and at the museum. Carrie knew this was a find. She wanted it. She'd get it, get it for John, to thank him for teaching her to recognize the seed in the weave, the releasing thread.

As she straightened, she covered it again with the ringed quilt. Had the Georgetown dealer noticed? Had he known? She wondered how this rug came to be here in a Pennsylvania farmhouse.

The auctioneer, finished with the heavy equipment, carried his portable microphone toward the barn. The group around him was mostly men, farmers. They bid carefully, inspecting the electric fence boxes, cables, tools. A few older men had on denim bib overalls, but most dressed casually for a nonworking day. John would have liked the old tools, the piles of harness, milking stools, and lanterns that had collected in the barn. Once when he had come with her, he'd brought home a dovetailed apple crate with odds and ends of hinges and coat hooks, but at the bottom he found a leather bag of Victorian marbles. The green glass held patterned swirls of thin colored lines and tiny bubbles. Carrie was delighted. She wanted them for a wooden tic-tac-toe game, but they seemed to trouble John, and he did an odd thing. He gave them to the young girl on the neighboring farm who sold the brown eggs they bought every Saturday at the roadside stand. Carrie said the child would never appreciate them, but the girl had been unexpectedly pleased by the gift.

Carrie spotted the Georgetown dealer. She was sure it was he trying the catch of an oak icebox. He had a trim beard, and his jeans, pressed and very clean, were held by a brass buckled belt. He carried a clipboard.

The auctioneer turned to the farm bell. It still hung on the shed near the kitchen door, tilted slightly with a bit of frayed rope, too high to reach. "It's a fine old bell from York foundry, I do believe."

A woman behind the food table wiped her hands on her apron and said to her assistant, "Rusty's going to try to get it for Grandma. She can take it with her, put it in Roy's shed even if they won't use it."

Carrie knew this happened at sales. Family or friends would buy back beloved treasures the auctioneer had persuaded the owners to sell or that they had been too numb to hold onto.

The auctioneer named a figure. Carrie saw the dealer run his eyes over the crowd. No one opened, the price was dropped. Then the young man with red hair raised his hand. The bidding started in fast, coming from various parts of the crowd, but after a bit, narrowed to the dealer and the young man Carrie assumed was Rusty. The dealer leaned against a tractor and to register his bid, nodded very slightly. Rusty raised his hand as if he were answering a question in school.

The price was getting high. At one point Rusty hesitated, looked up at the bell, then at the porch before he put up his hand. Back and forth between them. Suddenly the rhythm stopped, heads were turned toward the dealer, waiting. He was quiet, eyes down. The price was repeated, the man moved his head in a tiny negative gesture. The crowd turned back toward Rusty. Someone nudged him, and he held up his number. Later Carrie heard the woman behind the food table say to him, "It's all right, we'll help."

They were selling the furniture now. Carrie stopped by the food stand for a plastic cup of coffee and sat on the steps near a grey-haired man. Earlier she'd heard him tell Rusty to get the kids out of the barn loft; the hay went with the place, and they weren't doing it any good. Carrie wanted to talk with him, find out about the family. When he lit a cigarette, she pulled one from her purse and asked him for a light. He was pleased to talk. He'd been a neighbor all his life. The old lady was going to live with one of her sons. Good boys, nice families, too. They all have farms around here, better than this, the old home place.

"These hill farms can't make it; they haven't the acre-age—six-, seven-acre fields—and mostly on ledges, thin soil hardly worth fertilizing. No daughters, but plenty of grands. There was another boy, left home early during the Great Depression, worked migrant. He was a Japanese prisoner of war. We was set to give him a big welcome, but he never come back. Went to live in the west with some Indians. He died out there soon after. They say he was always her favorite."

He coughed lightly and was quiet for a bit, then lit another cigarette. The auctioneer moved to the kitchen things, and Carrie went off to bid. She loved this part. She'd wait to see where the bidding would start; she'd watch her competition, know her top price. She bought a butter crock and a blue granite colander with satisfactory weight and balance that made her aluminum one seem tacky. The old man talked to the woman in the chair who continued rocking as if to comfort a child.

At the far end of the porch, a man began to stack the folded blankets and curtains on a table, another picked the quilts off the railing leaving the rug exposed. Carried looked around for the dealer; surely he'd be interested. She had last

15

seen him carrying a box of plates and glasses to the parking area. He'd bought the best of the depression-ware and a number of odd lots that probably had one or two good pieces in them. She thought she'd seen an octagonal Wedgwood platter with a Chinese temple in one of the lots, but she hadn't looked closely. Had he noticed the rug? A pang went through her like pain, startling her with its force.

The bidding began with the curtains. Helpers held them up so you could see the faded folds, a ragged patch where a cat must have clawed. Carrie, distanced by the hum in her body, looked over the crowd to the field beyond. A car started, a green roof moved behind the bushes. Then the auctioneer nodded toward the rug as if to get it out of the way before selling the quilts.

"Here's an Indian saddle blanket," he said. "Who'll open?"

Someone behind her must have signaled. She waited but did not turn around. The bidding was slow. Carrie looked at the rug spread on the table, black and brown earth colors, the island of grey and the jagged red lightning. She knew its worth. There was a pause. She could hear the tension drop from the auctioneer's voice, thinking he had his final bid. As he swept his glance across the crowd, Carrie raised a finger. She did not take her eyes from him, she did not look behind her. The auctioneer swung his body toward her, then back toward the unseen bidder behind her. Surely it was the dealer in jeans nodding his bid. She heard a dry cough from the porch and a chair rocking. She raised her hand until the sound of the hammer and sudden silence. Carrie realized the silence came from a stilling of the rocker.

She held up her number and lifted the rug from the table. Its lightning streak hurt her eyes. She walked away fast without looking back to the porch. Around the corner, she stopped by the table to write her check but had to wait for the record sheets to be brought out. She stood with her back toward the house facing a round of flowers planted in beds made from tires cut with zigzag edges. Geraniums spilled out onto the earth. The old lady will have a handsome check, Carrie thought, and she'll have flower beds at her son's house. She pulled out a cigarette but could find no matches. When she pushed it back into the packet, it broke, spilling crumbs of tobacco into her purse.

16

The young woman came out with the sale sheets and silently punched her calculator; she did not look up when she took the check. As Carrie walked to the parking field, the rug felt stiff and heavy as canvas. The space beside her car was empty, the grass trampled flat around an untouched island between wheel marks.

Carrie felt sick. She had known who she was bidding against. But she'd done it for John. He would love the rug, besides, he would never have to know.

Late Summer Break

Ella set her traveling bag on the porch and looked across the yard into the shadowed interior of the barn where her husband was finishing the chores. At one point he crossed a cone of sun spreading through the open door; light caught on his work boots and his hand fisted to carry a water bucket. She could not see his face, but she'd recognize Howard's solemn walk anywhere, the way she could identify a red-tailed hawk in flight with only a glimpse at the edge of her eye.

They were leaving that day for a weekend on the Eastern Shore. It was the lull when the second-cutting hay was in and the corn wasn't yet ready for picking. In the past weeks, she had canned bushels of beans and tomatoes; her cellar shelves were lined with jars. Ella reckoned her harvest by the mason jars with handwritten labels: dill beans, pickles, strawberry jam. She'd go over the gleaming rows in her mind the way Howard used to go over the pedigrees of his milking herd. He'd read and reread their registered names as if to lock his good fortune into safety. The odd thing was he used to call the cows by other names: Maud, Flicker, Wobble; the bull was Old Bluff. Only the young steers he kept for market had no names.

Ella reached down to feel the soil of a potted begonia. She had arranged for her daughter-in-law, Janice, to water the houseplants and feed the cats while they were gone. Burt and Janice lived just down the road with the three kids, and Burt still helped on the farm when they needed him. Before he opened his TV repair shop, he used to work full-time with his father. Sometimes Ella thought Howard had Burt in mind when he shifted to beef cattle. They took a lot less work.

She pinched off a dead blossom and looked again toward the barn. This late summer break was her particular treat, and although she had to talk Howard into going every time, they rarely missed it. Today Howard was as slow as ever getting off. He'd been on the phone to the co-op about a baler part, then he called Burt to go over the chores again and tell him about the new fly spray although it was Burt suggested he try it.

Ella smoothed her skirt as Howard stomped up the steps.

"I'll go clean up," he said.

She went to collect her knitting, and when Howard came down with the suitcase, she was wiping dust off the car's dashboard.

They drove out on old Route 40 rather than the interstate. Ella liked the back roads that curved around hills and passed through small towns; she liked to see how people kept their houses, the way they painted their mailboxes or planted flowers in tires along the road. A woman pinning clothes on the line bent over in an easy motion then stretched up unfurling a blue sheet. Ella wondered how a stranger passing their farm would see her.

It was a dry year, the yarrow and early goldenrod along the road already dim with dust. From time to time she'd glance down at the baby blanket she was knitting. Janice was expecting again.

"Land's parched," Howard said.

"Clover's dying back. They're late cutting," she said.

"They'll make out," he said. "People do."

He sat straight, looking at the road, his head neat as a weathervane against the light, hands clamped to the wheel. His joints had begun to thicken with arthritis, and when he shifted gears his fingers moved in one piece. But he'd always driven upright, never easy like Burt with one arm stretched along the seat back. When they first went out together in his Model A pickup, Ella would try to make Howard look at her. She'd say something outrageous or touch his sleeve; he'd glance at her and then blink his eyes into a tight line. She didn't know for sure what it was he saw.

"Let's check into the motel first, and then walk down to where the crab boats are," he said.

Ella nodded. That's what they usually did. He liked watching the crates winched up onto the dock. Inside the slats, crabs would rustle and click; occasionally a flash of white glinted out from the dark blue mass.

"That sounds good," she said.

The sun reflected like a hazy moon through oxidized paint on the old Pontiac's hood.

"Burt never got to ride on one of them boats," Howard said.

Ella looked across the fields to the woods rolling back in heavy midsummer swells. "He would've if he'd joined the navy," she said.

"He was needed on the farm."

Ella knitted on without saying anything.

"He wanted change too fast, is all," Howard said.

"Too slow by his reckoning." Ella switched needles and started a new row.

She took a short breath to say something but then closed her mouth and pulled loose an arm's length of yarn.

"He's on his own now," Howard said.

A few days earlier, she had been on the porch with Burt waiting for Howard to come to dinner. He had been under the baler replacing a pin, and they'd watched him ease backward, rolling onto his knees; he'd used his hands to set his foot flat on the ground.

"The damned baler's worn out." Burt crossed his arms the way Ella sometimes did. "He can afford payments on a new one."

"Your father likes to pay for things whole," she said. "Give him time."

"Time! I gave him ten years, farming. He hardly knew I was there until I left. Now he comes to the shop and tells me I've got my tools hanging wrong. What does he want? Sometimes I don't think he even sees me."

Ella touched her fingers to her mouth and nodded. She knew about waiting for Howard to turn his head.

"Then he goes and deeds me the lower farm." Burt looked across the pasture toward the hollow where his house lay. "Hell, I don't know." He rubbed the back of his neck.

Howard slowed for an intersection. "We're almost there."

They had discovered the town one year on their way back from the beach. Burt, about four years old, had been cranky, and Ella, fed up with seafront crowds, was glad to see a place where people lived in an ordinary way. Howard

20

drove slowly down the main street with its wooden store-fronts set well back. "No parking meters," Howard said, then read a sign, "Crab House, all you can eat." They had followed the arrow pointing to a building by the inlet where the crab boats tied up. Burt had broken out of the car like a calf from a pen and run to the dock with Howard after him.

Thankful for a quiet moment, Ella set off on a narrow track along the marsh edge. It was raised from the wet ground and surfaced with oyster shells. Unfamiliar grasses grew in broad clumps, and red-winged blackbirds rode the stems calling to each other. When she turned to go back, the Crab House was a tiny square in the distance. Marshes stretched low and flat with no hills to cut them off. A sweep of pleasure caught her, and she spread her arms and spun around a couple of times before she walked back, giddy with the sweetness of the place.

They returned the following summer and in the years after until the milking barn burned. Ella turned the knitting on her lap and waited. Howard's face flickered again in her mind, and behind him orange snow streaked the night sky. He had smashed the siding on the barn's north end with an ax to reach the trapped herd, but flames twisted out along with the cries of the cattle. Then he battered through the east side, and when the trucks came, Jack Brimmer had to pull him back before the flaming rooftree bent in on itself. He shook Jack away and raised his fists as if he were separating iron bars.

By morning, the black ruins circled with snow steamed like an opening in the earth. Ella brought Howard coffee in a mug, and he drank it on the porch steps without speaking, staring all the while at the forsythia bush. During the night, heat had pulled tawdry yellow blooms from its branches. He silently handed her the empty mug and mounted the tractor to begin cleaning up. For weeks, he came home streaked black and smelling of charred wood. With the insurance money, he built a new barn, but not a milking barn. "Beef is a living," he said.

They had come to the main street. "Traffic signal's new," Howard said.

A few blocks further on, they turned into the motel, a

low building with the parking lot in front and open fields behind.

"They gave it a paint job this year." Howard pulled in by the office.

"And fancy new prices, I'll bet," Ella said.

Crossing to the office, Howard pressed his hand against his hip and slowly straightened. Ella rolled her knitting into a towel and patted her hair. Through the glass door, she could see Howard sway back on his heels and rub his chin as he talked to the woman behind the desk. He had something to decide, the price probably. He came out and leaned down to the open window on her side, his eyes bright and very blue.

"They have only one room left," he said. "It has a water bed."

"A water bed?"

"They're comfortable, the woman says. I'll fetch the cases." Howard held out the key. "Number nine, at the end."

As she unlocked the door, Ella smiled. He'd already taken the room. A water bed. The room was dark after the bright sun; it smelled of used air. She pulled back the curtains made of a soft red material. The bed was huge, a red velvet plain with a mound of pillows by the headboard. That was red, too. She snapped on the air-conditioning and the fan hoping to bring fresh air into the room; Howard set the bags on the luggage rack.

"Well, what do you think?" He touched the coverlet gingerly, his fingers spread like the poles of a tepee.

Ella hitched up her skirt and sat on the edge. A board cut under her knees. She lay back stretching her arms out; the bed gave, then drew up, raising her in a slow wave. Water gurgled close to her ear.

"I didn't think it would make noise," she said.

"You look like you're floating."

"That's what I am doing." Ella sat up and laughed. "What would Burt and Janice think?"

"They won't know if you don't tell them."

Howard combed his hair in front of the bathroom mirror. He parted it carefully, then wet the comb and slicked it sideways, the way he did when they first met.

"Let's go," he said.

They walked on the shady side of the street, slowly passing houses and shops: Murphy's, an IGA grocery, Union

Mission thrift shop. Howard paused by the hardware store to look at a display of anchors, pulleys, bait buckets, and tools Ella did not recognize.

"Solid brass, those pulleys," he said.

At the lower end of the street, shops gave way to shingled storage sheds, and as they turned the corner, Ella had the view she'd been waiting for. The pavement ended at the water's edge with a row of heavy wooden posts and crab boats tied to them. Marshes lay beyond the inlet, then a strip of blue water and a stand of distant trees that barely thickened the horizon's line. Ella breathed the smell of tar and salt and iron. Sometimes on the farm she'd catch a drift of creosote, and her mind would fill with the feel of this place. She remembered how familiar it seemed the first time—as if she were already connected to it.

Everything was well used—the posts grooved and shiny where ropes wound round them, and tires, frayed to the fiber, hung as bumpers along the boats' sides. Men wore rubber boots and loose overalls; their hands would be callused on the sides where they hauled in fishing lines. Crabbing was dirty work, different from farming, different dirt. She watched a young man, bare to the waist, heft a metal ice chest over the deck of a boat. That dip and shift underfoot would take getting used to.

A woman about Ella's age passed a cloth-covered basket across the gap of water to a man leaning from the boat. He said something to make her laugh, and she tapped him on the arm. Ella would like to talk with that woman, find out what she put in the basket for his dinner. She could pack sandwiches and a thermos of coffee for her husband, too. She could learn the names of ropes and tools and how to slope her weight against the waves. She looked over at Howard. He'd be stiff as a bottle standing on a boat that moved under him.

"Hey," she said. "Where are the crabs you promised me?"

"I'm watching them." A man at the far end of the wharf carried a crate through the door of the wooden building with Crab House painted on its roof.

The restaurant hadn't changed much since they first came, the same folding wooden chairs and sawbuck tables covered with brown wrapping paper. A piece of board was set in front of each place, and in the center of the table, a mug held little wooden bats and sticks for picking out the meat. They took a table by the big window overlooking the marshes and sat facing each other. A letter board by the door listed the different kinds of crab and side dishes you could order. The prices were in red.

"They have jumbos," Howard said.

"We've always had regulars."

"I thought to try the jumbos." Howard was reading the menu, frowning a little.

"Let's try them."

Ella didn't often sit across from Howard like this. At home she'd be to one side of the table where she could serve from the stove. On days when Burt came to help, he'd eat with them and sometimes a grandchild, but mostly it was just the two of them. For a moment, with him across from her like that, Ella wondered what they'd talk about while they ate.

The waitress brought a hill of crabs on a tin tray. Ella dropped one on the board and banged the shell with a wooden bat. She knew where to dig for the meat.

Howard recalled the first time Burt tasted crabs. "He caught on fast enough," he said. "Broke his record every year."

"I'd never seen a whole cooked crab before," she said. "I watched the people at the next table to learn how to get them apart."

"I was doing the same."

"We never let on to Burt."

"Or to each other." Howard took a pull of his beer, and they worked their jumbo crabs, teasing out hunks of white meat.

"They're good," Ella said.

Howard was looking past her, his hand curled half-closed on the table as if he'd just lifted it off the steering wheel.

"The table's too wide for that young couple," he said.

Ella twisted around and saw them leaning toward each other as if they were looking in a mirror. The girl's hair fell forward onto her arms.

"And the clock's too slow," he said.

"There's time enough," Ella said, "but they don't know that yet."

She turned back; Howard was still watching them.

"It's their beginning," Ella said softly, "a sweet time."

Howard swung his head toward the window, closing his eyes slow and easy. "I get thinking," he said. "Things work out sometimes. Look at us. Look at Burt. He's done good, considering."

The waitress set down their coffee and took a handful of cream packets from her apron pocket. Howard held one in his palm. "Doesn't seem hardly worth it, these little things. Remember them twenty-gallon cans? They'd ring and clang in the pickup bed. Chimes, I used to call them." He shook his head. "No more cans. It's all automatic now, done with tanks and hose connections. I don't even know the names of the things."

"You know my name."

He looked up fast, like a buck in the meadow. "Yes. Ella. Your name is Ella."

She turned to the window. Why had she said that? The sun was low, its gold light caught on tufts of grass, raking streaks of shadow across the marsh. They drank their coffee and watched a pair of gulls fly with heavy strokes toward the bay.

By the time they left, color had gone from the sky, and the boats at anchor were separated by silver water. A street lamp came on dimming inlet and marsh. As they walked back to the motel, Ella could make out the Big Dipper tilting over the trees.

"Think we'll sleep good in that water bed?" she said.

"Not right off, I hope." Howard reached for her hand. She wondered if he could feel the warm hollow between their palms through his calluses.

He unlocked the door. Ella switched on the light and pulled the curtains shut. For a moment, the walls of the room closed her off from everything familiar: the night, the sound of trees; even Howard, leaning over the table, seemed a stranger in the pink light.

"There's instructions how to use the bed," he said.

Ella folded her dress over a chair. "I never known you to take a lesson in going to bed."

He smiled and unbuttoned his shirt. "You just get in there now."

She lay down on the bed and let its motion quiet. At home Howard would sit on the edge of their high bed and swing his legs up, but this was low and he knelt onto it,

25

pushing himself forward. The mattress swayed under him.

"You can't get purchase on this thing," he said.

"Lie still a bit. You'll get used to it."

He settled beside her and took her hand. "A poor job of covering a leak." He was looking up at a piece of shiny metal flashing, flat as glass taped to the ceiling over the bed. Ella had read once how sometimes there was a mirror, so you could watch yourself. Howard didn't know.

"This place is built cheap," he said. "Even the door is hollow."

At home their solid oak doors carried generations of paint.

They talked and floated, neither of them moving. Ella listened to the pauses, the time it took to reach back and circle a patched leak, a painted door, a summer picnic. Each thing they spoke of trailed threads fine and tough as cobwebs. Then Howard shifted a little, his arm pressed against her, pulled back and pressed in again. He squeezed her hand.

"Hey. My girl."

He rolled toward Ella and ran his hand across her breasts, his fingers limber on her body. Maybe they had curved to fit her rather than the tractor's wheel. The thought pleased Ella, and so did the motion of the bed. It seemed to isolate each move in a kind of stately rise and dip; sometimes it pulled them apart and they held for a moment, air flowing between them, cooling her skin, before they folded back together again.

Later Howard said, "I like riding the water with you, Ella." He lay against her, and without moving his head, kissed her neck. He would sleep now.

The sound of water subsided, and Ella opened her eyes, uncertain if the bed was still moving. On the ceiling, framed by strips of masking tape, was the image of a woman. From a swirl of red cloth, her shining thighs rose and rounded to the stretch of her back; her upper body curved in, and her arms circled the head of a sleeping man. His face was in shadow, but a strand of his grey hair fell across her breast, and her fingers lightly touched his temple.

She's minding him, Ella thought, holding him, as water would hold him, above his discontent. She pulled her arms closer around Howard. The image on the ceiling rose and withdrew like a boat tied to the dock. She looked into the eyes of the woman. This is what Howard sees. This is me, Ella.

For an instant, she felt herself gleam as if a coating of dust had washed away. Clear as the silence following a blackbird's song, she knew she would always live among hills with tools she could name.

The Fall Rise

North of Albany where the foothills begin to take on mass and rock ledges edged with evergreen rise from the highway, I watched for the first glimpse of the blue Adirondack peaks. A drift of pine through the open window startled a surge of expectation. I've been coming this way for thirty years, still that first whiff of north woods has power to stir; this year it's mixed with a wave of irritation. I'd cut short a stay at the beach to spend the second week of my vacation with my mother. It was the first summer in almost forty years she'd be at the lake without Pop.

Late in the afternoon, I pulled up under pines behind the cottage. I stood a moment taking in the familiar scene. The day was heavy with heat, and through the trees, the lake reflected sky the color of aluminum. The place was shabbier than I remembered—green lichen I hadn't noticed before brushed the cabin's shingles, and paint around the windows was peeling. Usually by August, the wooden half barrels that we gave Pop and Ma on their thirty-fifth anniversary were overflowing with nasturtiums, but this year they held only clumps of dried grass.

I followed the pine needle path around to the front of the house. Aunt Dee, my mother's younger sister, was sitting on the porch steps smoking, her grey hair pulled back by a scarf. A spinster. The word fits her—small and fine boned, but tough in her way. A librarian. She holds her elbows close to her sides as if trying to take up minimum space.

"Hi." I hugged her narrow shoulders.

"Laurie, you're a welcome sight." She pushed me to arm's length, then put her hand against my cheek. "You're the spitting image of your mother back then."

"Where is she?"

"In the kitchen getting dinner."

"How's it been?"

Aunt Dee shrugged. "I don't know. She doesn't do anything, not even fish; she just sits on the porch and reads mystery novels. She did make a bunch of pies for the Fourth of July bake sale. She and Mary McCray. They were always good friends. Sometimes she'll stop in the village and talk with Mary at the store; it's the only time she seems to connect. But I got her to cook, at least she does that. Then the weather's been awful, lots of rain."

Ma came out the door. "Thought I heard someone."

I had the odd sense of watching a stilled scene: a tall grey woman standing in the doorway of an aging summer cottage, hands pushed into the pockets of a barbecue apron, behind her, a deer skull on the wall and a gnawed beaver stick resting on a row of rusty nails. But the distance did not hold. Ma took her hands from her apron and touched me lightly on the arm. I kissed her cheek.

"How are you doing?" As soon as I spoke the words, they seemed intrusive.

"Hot." She pushed a strand of hair from her forehead with the back of her wrist.

My mother is part of this place—she's been coming here since she was born—and the place is part of her life. She always seemed to be different here, more content. Maybe it was the presence of her childhood. And she was different with Pop here, too; they shared a kind of gaiety, a secret pleasure with each other. They'd spend hours fishing or hiking in the high peaks. We'd go with them when we were kids, but I often felt they preferred being alone.

Last summer I wasn't around when Pop began to cough and lose weight; by the time I saw him over Labor Day he was a wraith. They had talked about staying on through September, but the doctor said he needed to go to the city for tests. That weekend, Ma and I put the blankets away in the mouse-proof tin boxes, cleaned the stove, and packed the perishable food in cartons to carry back to the city. Pop had always left a supply of wood ready by the fireplace and insisted on splitting the kindling even though he had to rest every few minutes. It took him all morning. Meanwhile, Ma and I pulled the boat up into the shed. When Pop came round the house and saw we had the boat stored in its place on the sawhorses, he stood without speaking, hands hanging loose, clothes too big for him. "That was my job," he said and turned away. Ma watched him walk down to the lake's edge where he leaned against a birch tree looking out at the mountains beyond.

All last fall, I drove the two hundred miles every other weekend to visit with him. It wasn't easy; I was working and taking law classes at night, but I wanted to be there. Ma needed someone to spell her, but even brittle with fatigue, she fought every inch of the way when I tried to get home-nursing help. Sometimes I felt my arrival interrupted a private conversation between them, that they politely tolerated my presence but were waiting for me to go. In spite of that, I'm glad for the time; I came to know Pop in new ways. I learned that anger and gratitude can exist side by side. On the long drives, I could push aside the press of daily life and be alone with Pop. I began to count on that solitary time driving through the dark, not thinking, but letting myself feel angry, sad, and grateful.

He died in January. Ma managed fine over the funeral and the weeks following, but when I came back for midwinter break, she seemed to have shrunk; her voice had gone flat. She'd sit for hours not even reading. The place was clean enough, but the refrigerator was almost empty, the magazines too neatly arranged. The house had lost color. Ma always had geraniums blooming in the window, even in winter. When I asked about the absence of flowers, she said she forgot to water them.

Nick came out from the West Coast that same weekend, and we both recognized the weight of Ma's loneliness. The two of us drove across town to talk with Aunt Dee. We sat in her sunny kitchen drinking coffee. "One of her friends drops in at least once a day, and we talk every evening," Aunt Dee said. "She'll get through this all right. It takes time."

"This summer she'll need someone with her," Nick said. "I can come for a long weekend, drive her up and stay over to put the boat in and see to the firewood. She can't be alone there."

"Why not?" Aunt Dee said.

"She doesn't have Pop."

Aunt Dee never married, but Ma was by herself for the

first time in years.

We would arrange for friends to visit at the lake. Aunt Dee usually spent part of her vacation there, and I volunteered to cover the last week of August.

"You sure this is what your mother wants?" Aunt Dee asked as she stamped out a cigarette. "Could be she wants time by herself."

I looked at Nick. "She shouldn't be by herself," I said.

The heat hung on after Aunt Dee left, one sultry day after another. On my last afternoon, Ma and I sat on the porch still waiting for a break in the weather. Mosquitoes, usually gone by August, swarmed off the water; the screened porch was the only place we could be outside without their fine whine circling our heads. I lay in the hammock, pressing my foot against the shingles in a slow rhythm and thinking of my paralegal job and the start of night classes. When I'm on vacation, I forget about work until just before I have to go back, then anxiety pours in.

Air lay thick as a mist over the lake. Ma, in her Adirondack chair, read a paperback. The glass of iced tea she'd set on the flat arm sweated a puddle of water around it. From time to time, she leaned back to tweak her shirt away from her neck and blow down her front.

"Hot," she said. "It never used to be this hot at the end of August."

"Remember the year it snowed, and we were late for school?"

The Saturday before Labor Day, we'd always get ready to close the cottage and leave early on Sunday. Although it would be late when we reached home, we'd have the holiday to get ready for school. One year, we woke to a blizzard and had to hunker down in the cottage for two days before the plow came through to open the road. It was amazing to see the place in snow. Pop brought in armfuls of wood and kept the fire going. We had to unpack the blankets. Ma made meals of soup and canned macaroni left from the summer, and at night we played hearts in front of the fire. Ma said as a girl she'd been envious of her friend Mary McCray who lived here all year round. Mary had told her about fishing through the ice and how she'd have to snowshoe to school.

"I love the first cold nights," Ma said. "The sharp edge. You look out one morning and the swamp maples are purple."

"No fear of that this year."

"Your father and I often talked about staying on after the weather turned. That's when the trout come to the surface— the fall rise." Ma looked out at the lake. "We never did."

"You didn't fish this summer."

"Nick took a couple trout when he was here."

"But you and Pop went out every evening."

"It's what I did with your father."

"You taught me, remember?"

I was eight and learning to row. Ma had come with me while I splashed the oars and spun the boat in circles. She cast her line out, but didn't complain when I bumped the shore or took her among the lily pads. When she hooked a trout, she handed the bending rod to me.

"Here, you bring it in."

I took hold and felt the fish tug, felt it alive and fighting.

"Keep the rod up, the line tight," Ma said. A slick curve broke the water; the line went slack, the fly bounced back, and my hand felt a sudden emptiness.

"It's gone."

"That's OK," she said, "you'll get another."

She showed me how to cast—pull the rod up sharp, pause, then bring the tip down and let the line carry out. I practiced over and over. By the end of the summer, I could drop a fly within inches of an underwater rock. She taught me to wait a split second when a trout went for the fly before the jerk to set the hook.

This year I couldn't get her onto the lake. "Later," she said. "It's too hot. The fish are at the bottom where the water's cold."

I got her to take a few walks, once to pick raspberries, but the mosquitoes were so bad we came back with only a handful of berries in our cans. Ma spent hours reading, conversation seemed an effort, yet at the general store she would chat for twenty minutes with Mary McCray. I'd wait in the car with the newspaper while they talked, leaning against the checkout counter.

"You're staying till the end of the week?" The hammock made a soft thump each time it swung against the wall. "I start work on Tuesday."

"Iris will help me close the cabin."

"Iris?"

"Iris McCray, Mary's daughter. She works at Sears in Glen's Falls. She'll come on the weekend."

I knew Iris, a lumpy overweight girl who used to work with her mother in the store. I hadn't seen her in ages. Why should I be nettled that Ma would ask her to help? After all, I had to get back. Maybe Ma was ready for me to leave, waiting for me to leave.

I swung my feet off the hammock. "You know, I haven't been fishing all week."

Ma looked over her half glasses, "Take my rod. It's in the closet," she said, "and Pop's brown creel."

I stopped in the doorway. "Come with me," I said.

Ma set her book face down on the chair arm and turned toward the lake. Clouds had begun to collect over the mountain as they had every afternoon since I'd been here, but today they piled high and hard-edged. "We better go now if we're going," she said, "there's weather coming."

As I walked down to the dock, I again had the momentary sense of seeing my mother from a distance: a woman in jeans standing alone on the silvered planks of a dock facing a silent lake circled by forest.

The flat-bottomed scow hadn't been used for some time, and a spider had built a complex web across the oars. I dropped the creel next to the stern seat; Ma settled on the front thwart, untied the rope from the iron ring, and pushed off. The water seemed dark, almost sullen; heat shimmered over the marsh by the outlet. Except for a quiver of insects on the surface, the lake was still. We drifted while Ma set the oars in the locks, and I fitted together the bamboo rod. I pulled an arm's length of line off the reel. The sound made me think of Pop; he would stand in the boat and screech out yards of line, his cast catching the low sun in a big S curve over his head.

Ma rowed with casual competence, and barely glancing over her shoulder, took us across the lake to where a small freshet greened the grass. She had told me to look for such a place; the fish lie where cool water flows in. She rested the oars; the boat glided parallel to the shore. I finished tying on the leader.

"I forgot the net," I said.

"Nothing's moving," Ma said.

I whipped the air a few times to get my line out, then laid a fly beside a fallen log. Almost at once a swirl broke the water. I hadn't expected a rise and jerked the line too fast. I flicked the fly again over the same spot. Another surge, this time I remembered the split second wait. The trout hit, the rod bent and the reel sang out, then nothing—a dead weight on the line.

Ma leaned over the side as if she could see down. "It's sulking," she said, "they sometimes do."

"I think I snagged bottom." But as I spoke, a tug carried to my hand. "It's there."

I eased the rod back, but the line went slack, and twenty feet from the boat a trout, bigger than any I had ever seen, rose clear out of the water. It dove, and the line zizzed off the reel. I pushed the tension button on full, but it didn't slow the spin. Then the run stopped.

"Keep your line tight." Ma edged the boat away from shore.

As I reeled in, I felt the fish twist before it dove again, then another ratchet back, another run. Each dive carried the fish a lesser distance, with less speed.

"How can we land it?" I'd seen Pop beach a trout, but here alders grew right to the lake's edge.

"Let it tire. When it's ready, bring it alongside, I'll hook it under the gills."

"Can you?"

"Your father showed me how," she said. "Jigging, he called it."

The line sloped into a glare of reflected sky. The trout's back broke the water in a slow roll.

"It's almost ready," I said.

I lifted the rod, working the fish in close to the boat. Ma bent forward, her whole body intent as she lowered her hand into the water. The trout, barely moving except for the fanning red gills, floated on its side, exposing a row of blue speckles and pink underbelly.

"It's huge," Ma whispered. Her hand moved up fast, and for an instant she held the fish above the water, but it twisted away in a slick mottled curve. My rod sprung loose, the line flapped.

"Damn," Ma said. "I almost had it." She raised her hand to her nose. "I can smell it, smell the lake bottom."

"The leader broke." I caught the shirred nylon end.

"He always said the big ones were here," Ma said.

As I reeled in, a press of air swung the boat around. "Hey, we better get back," I said.

The sky had darkened with fast moving clouds; wind riffled the trees, flipping the birch leaves silver side up. Ma turned the scow and started across the lake pulling hard against the oars. The wind picked up; small waves slapped the floor boards, and before we reached the dock, rain hit. By the time we had moored the boat and slithered up the path to the house, we were soaked. We dropped our gear on the porch and stood breathing hard in the sudden calm. Rain had obliterated the lake. I realized I was cold.

"Go take a hot shower," Ma said. "I'll get tea."

Twenty minutes later in dry clothes, I found the fire lit and Ma in Pop's red wool wrapper seated at the table. She had his fly book open in front of her and a mug of tea beside it. "Your tea's on the counter," she said.

I carried the mug to the bench in front of the fire. "I'll take the rod down later," I said.

"Don't bother. I've hung it on the porch."

"But I leave tomorrow."

"I don't." She threaded a leader through the eye of a brown and red Montreal. "Your father must have put this away wet. The hooks have rusted through the nylon. That's why your fly snapped."

She coiled the leader and secured it with a twist of tie wire. "It'll be clear in the morning; you'll have a good day to drive back."

"And you leave next Sunday?"

"No. I'm staying on." She tucked the looped nylon into a plastic envelope. "With this cold front moving through, to-morrow the trout will be stirring."

She slid the fly book into the creel hanging on the back of her chair. "I'll have to get out my lumber jacket."

Her voice had a resonance I hadn't heard in months.

"You'll be glad to be alone, won't you?" I said.

Ma leaned toward me. "You were good to come, Laurie,

you and Dee and Nick, but it's time I landed a trout by my-self." She sat back and looked around the room. "Besides, this is where I want to be."

Aunt Dee had been right; Ma was waiting for us to go. I remembered my solitary night drives. I thought of Ma stand-ing on the dock, and how she bent to jig the trout, and for the first time this summer, she was fully present. She pushed back from the table and stretched, the red wrapper falling from her thin arms.

"That's more than I've done all summer," she said. "It's good to be tired."

Rain thrummed on the roof, the fire hissed, and we crossed the edge into fall.

Floyd

Rosa, carrying a half bale of straw, crossed from bright fall sun into shadow at the north end of the barn. The air was still there, stagnant, and the sudden cold felt like a draft. When they bought the farm ten years before, a cowhide had been nailed skin-side out against the weathered boards. The smell of the desiccating hide seemed to hang on, mixing with the rank must of burdock and nettles. Rosa usually avoided passing that way, but it was the shortest route from the barn to the raspberry beds.

Emerging from the shade, she was glad for the sun on her shoulders as she scattered straw mulch between the canes, settling it around the stems with a fork. A blue pickup pulled in by the house and gave two short honks. Rosa straightened, pushing back a strand of hair. Belle, her neighbor, waved from the cab.

"Hey, Rosa, is Frank around?"

It was too far to talk without shouting. Rosa stuck the fork in the ground and started up the hill watching her feet on the uneven path. She stopped beside the truck. Belle, her face fringed with white hair, leaned on her elbow; a hole in her sweater exposed a ragged circle of flowered print shirt.

"Frank's in town," Rosa said, "getting snow tires." She spoke in small bursts on her outgoing breath. "Is there anything I can tell him?"

"Floyd Trask is laying in the road, and I can't move him," Belle said.

"Oh," Rosa said. Floyd lived in a shack past Belle and Pete's farm, and he'd startled Rosa more than once when she'd come on him sleeping his wine off by the side of the road or under the bridge where the exit comes off the interstate.

"Could I help?" she asked.

Belle put a hand to her chin and assayed Rosa as she

would a farmhand wanting work.

"Sure," she said. "We'll manage."

Rosa walked round the front of the pickup tucking in her shirt, pleased that Belle had called on them. She climbed into the cab and slid across the cracked seat while Belle held Buster, the overfed terrier that went everywhere with her. Belle started the truck; Buster balanced his hindquarters on Rosa's knees and spread his front paws on the dashboard. Rosa put a hand on his back to steady him as they turned onto the tarmac. The movements of the truck were larger than she was used to in her car, the view wider.

Belle frowned slightly as she drove. They had been summer neighbors for a decade, but only in the last year since Rosa and Frank moved to their farm year-round had they become friends. Rosa would walk through the woods to Belle's farm; they'd sit in the kitchen drinking coffee and chatting while Belle crocheted squares in bright acrylic yarn. She would tell Rosa about her life on the farm, about how she and Pete weathered hard times. They talked about local news, the lack of rain, and when to set out seedlings.

The farm, too, connected them. It had belonged to Belle's uncle before Frank and Rosa bought it. "I've walked every corner," she said, then shook her head. "But there's always a place I haven't come on yet. That's the pleasure of it."

An old cart track ran through the woodlot between the two farms, and Belle's husband, Pete, still used it when he cut their meadows. In exchange for the hay, he kept an eye on their place when they were in the city. Pete, who was sharp that way, had suggested the arrangement before Frank knew the price of hay. But it had worked out. Pete still cut their fields and hunted over their land in deer season.

Their first autumn on the farm, Rosa planned to post the land and had walked the line identifying the witness trees marked with horizontal blazes. On one of her explorations, she broke out of the woods through low-growing sumac onto the meadow and almost walked into a pickup. A heavy-set man wearing an orange hunting cap sat on the fender with a gun across his knees. She was so close she did not immediately recognize him.

"Oh, it's you, Pete," she said. "You surprised me." She moved a few steps back. "I'm glad you didn't mistake me for a deer."

"I knew who it was all right," he said. His close-set eyes watched her; he shook his beer can as if to check how much was left. Rosa looked away across the meadow.

"You get a fine view here."

"I shot my first buck down there," Pete pointed with his thumb still watching her. "And plenty others since."

"I guess you've hunted here for a long time."

"That's right."

"We don't mind you hunting here, really. It's strangers we don't want."

"Good," Pete said, "that's what I figured."

Rosa had intended to walk home across the field, but instead turned back into the woods. They did not post the land.

Belle held her hand to shade her eyes against the low sun.

"What happened to Floyd?" Rosa asked.

Belle closed her mouth with a half smile. "I was going to the co-op for freezer paper. Pete's fixing to butcher hogs this week, and you know where the road rises up steep and all you see is sky over the hood? Well, I come to the top, and he's laying there right across the road. Takes the breath out of me. I pull up sharp onto the grass, not sure I missed him until I got out."

The truck crossed back into the trees.

"He hasn't the sense to lay to the side," Belle said. "I gave him a push with my foot to see if he'd wake, but he's out cold, still holding his wine bottle like someone was going to take it. You wouldn't believe that skinny wisp of a man was so resisting. When I tried to roll him over, he wouldn't budge; his head lolled back like a dead calf's. I couldn't leave him laying there. I remembered Pete keeps a flare under the front seat. I set it up in the road so's you can see it either way. Then I come for Frank."

"I'm glad someone was home," Rosa said.

Belle kept one hand firmly on the wheel. "Let's hope no fool came along too fast to stop."

"There's not much traffic," Rosa said.

Belle was leaning forward. "It's just up here, he is." At the top of the rise against the sky, the flare's magenta flame gleamed like neon in the muted landscape. A young woman was walking in front of it moving her arms in circles as if signaling far out at sea. Belle cut the engine and let the truck roll toward the flare. The woman came to the window.

"There's a man in the road," she said. "He's been hit. Someone hit him and left him here."

"Someone set out a flare because they couldn't move him," Belle said. She climbed down from the cab.

"Oh, it was you?"

"It was me lit the flare all right," Belle said. "It was the bottle hit him."

Rosa walked over to where Floyd lay in the center of the road diagonally across the solid yellow line. He was on his side with his knees bent as Rosa herself might sleep. The red plaid of his jacket was faded to pink across the shoulders, and his work boots rested one on top of the other in neat alignment. In contrast to his skin, which looked as if it were stained with walnut hulls, his eyelashes were pale. His imitation leather aviator's helmet lined with fleece flapped out like lamb's ears.

Rosa often saw Floyd in the village. In summer, he'd sit on the curb of the A & P parking lot with a basket of berries or wild mushrooms. After he sold them, he'd buy a jug of wine and walk the three miles back to his place. All last winter, he wore a woman's long black coat held closed with a rope, its fur collar turned up against his face like a refugee from Stalingrad. Rosa pointed him out to visitors as a local character, but she never bought his berries.

The first time she saw Floyd was through the window of the Goodwill store. She'd glanced at the display window, and deeper inside, past a rack of coats, an unshaven old man stood by a bin sorting through the used clothes, pushing them apart carefully as if searching the grass for a bird's nest. He held up a shirt and looked out straight at her. Rosa had felt as if she had been caught trespassing. His eyes, bright as nail heads, made no accommodation for her; she was a stranger here, unconnected to the town or the people, a poacher herself. The man bent again to winnow the clothes, and Rosa felt she'd glimpsed a strange landscape between freight cars. She had turned away and pulled her sweater close around her.

After that, whenever she saw Floyd walking ahead of her

in the direction she was driving, Rosa's thoughts would scatter. She'd reach for reasons why she couldn't pick him up: there was no room with the groceries, Frank was waiting for the paper. Once she surprised herself by saying aloud, "I'm sorry I can't, I just can't."

Later that summer, she and Frank were driving home through the rain, and Floyd was walking on the verge with a black plastic trash bag wrapped around him. He didn't turn around, simply held out his hand—not his thumb, his whole hand—as if he were reaching to greet someone. Frank stopped and opened the rear door. Floyd shook out the plastic.

"Much obliged," he said.

He sat with his knees together, the plastic folded in his lap. The smell of wine and damp wool filled the car. Rosa, aware of the two men and the close dank air, concentrated on the wipers' beat and the hiss of wheels on wet road.

Frank remarked on the rain.

"Good for mushrooms," Floyd said.

At the lane to Floyd's place, Frank stopped the car and turned, his arm over the back of the seat. "Stay dry," he said. Both men laughed. Rosa watched craters of rain break against the glass; she heard the shatter of plastic shaken loose. She knew Floyd was waiting and Frank, too. A draft of fragmented drops blew across her neck through the open door. She turned and nodded to Floyd. He smiled, and she looked past him into the shining woods.

"Much obliged," he said.

He never signaled to her again, and she never picked him up. But Frank did. Rosa would catch his smell, and Frank would say, "Yes, I gave old Floyd a lift."

Floyd's cheek was pressed against the road; Rosa wondered if the smell of tar crossed into his sleep.

"My husband has gone for help," the woman said. "He told me to stay here and warn cars."

"Floyd won't hurt no cars," Belle said. She had started toward the truck. "I'll back alongside; we can load him over the tailgate."

"You can't move him," the woman said.

Belle and Rosa looked at her. She was standing on the grass at the side of the road in a neat jacket and grey pants; a pretty scarf around her neck blew over the collar of her coat.

Her gloves were leather, pigskin. She folded her hands together and bent her wrists back like a child.

"You mustn't move him until help comes."

"Well, help has come," Belle said. She climbed into the truck, pushed Buster aside, and, looking over her right shoulder, backed around toward Floyd. Rosa motioned to guide Belle with small pulls of her hands. She watched the space close, then turned her palm out flat.

"OK," she called.

Belle set the brake and switched the engine off. She came around to unhook one side of the tailgate; Rosa undid the other.

"Don't move him. Richard is coming. My husband is bringing help," the woman said.

"If he went for the rescue squad, they'll be a time yet," Belle said. "Howard Strathmeyer can't start a pinochle hand without finishing it."

Rosa, aware of the woman watching them, pushed the spare tire deeper into the bed of the truck. The woman's presence seemed to give weight to every move.

"There, that's space enough," Rosa said.

"Reach me the sacking," Belle said. Rosa pulled forward a pile of burlap. Floyd looked limp as a sleeping child.

"Think we can manage?" Rosa said.

"We'll try," Belle said. "Turn him on his back, we'll set him up against the tailgate."

"What if something's broken?" The woman stayed well back from them.

"There's nothing broke in Floyd."

Belle shook out a sack and laid it flat on the road. They both leaned down on one side of him. Rosa slipped her hand under his arm, but, startled by the warmth of his body, she pulled away and drew in her breath. She glanced at Belle, then at her hand, before she returned it for a deeper grip. Together they rolled him on his back. A dark patch spread out on the road, and the powerful smell of urine rose around them.

"We'll work the burlap under him," Belle said. They tugged the sack until it was under his buttocks, then, one on each side, tried to lift him. He slipped, and they had to sit him up again.

"You can't treat him like that," the woman said. She moved along the verge a few strides and then back as if she were inside a fence. Belle and Rosa ignored her as they bent for another try.

"He's not an animal," the woman said.

Belle looked up sharply, her face flushed.

"They'll lock him up like one if we leave him," she said. "If you gave us a hand, it might not be so messy."

The woman stopped pacing and raised her head. She pulled the skin of her gloves tight, spread her fingers, and stepped forward. Rosa could see her looking at the wet stain on Floyd's pants.

"Grab ahold of his legs," Belle said, "under the knees. We'll lift him together."

The woman moved in close to Floyd. She squatted down. Rosa watched her face, but the woman reached around his legs without wincing and grasped them firmly. Belle counted, and they heaved. Floyd's body slumped; his weight pulled the three women together so they were almost touching. They held, breathing hard, their heads close, then Belle nodded her chin upward. They strained back and lifted him onto the bed of the truck. Floyd's legs dangled down, one arm bent at an awkward angle to his body. Belle pushed herself onto the truck bed so she was sitting beside him, and, reaching back, lifted his arm and laid it on his belly. She let her hand rest on his as the woman raised his legs and swung them onto the floor. His hat had fallen on the ground, and the woman stooped with an easy swing to pick it up. She brushed it against her knee and pulled her gloves off to untangle a twig enmeshed in the fleece. Belle raised Floyd's head for the woman to set the cap in place, then drew a sack under it as a pillow.

"That'll keep his head from banging," Belle said as she let herself down to the ground.

She hooked the tailgate. Rosa rubbed her hands along the seam of her jeans then crossed over and snuffed out the flare with her foot. The woman had moved to the edge of the road, and as Belle came round to the cab, she pointed to the wine jug in the grass. The three of them stood for a moment looking down at the green bottle.

Belle leaned over and picked it up. "He'll need it when he comes round." She turned to the woman. "Obliged for your help," she said.

The woman put her hands in her pockets, straightened her elbows, and smiled briefly. "I suppose they'll want to know where he is."

"They'll know, all right," Belle said. She closed the door and started the engine. "C'mon, Rosa."

Buster wriggled onto Rosa's knees, marking time with his feet. For a moment, Belle leaned against the seat, her body slack, her hand on the knob of the gear shift, then she straightened up and started the engine.

"She'll have that outfit to the cleaners, I'll bet."

Rosa glanced at her hands. She was rubbing them against Buster's rough back.

"I hope they leave him be," Belle said as she turned the truck and headed back. "Last year they took him to a detox center clean out of the county. Had him in a van. When they stopped to unload, he took off across the parking lot into the woods. Was back here a couple of days later to feed his animals. Said he couldn't stay in no rest home."

"You're a good friend to him, Belle."

"We was in school together. He lived in the hollow, same as he does now, him and his sister and his daddy. His mother died when he was little. They buried her in the family graveyard under the hemlocks. Cut through roots thick as my arm I remember. We'd walk to school together, Floyd and me and his sister."

"How did he make a living?" Rosa asked.

"Oh, he worked seasonal, picking apples, road crew. Now he has food stamps and a check. Lives to himself mostly, but he likes his wine."

Rosa looked back through the rear window. Floyd seemed to stir. His hands moved lightly as a dog might twitch a foot in sleep. A bright yellow leaf caught for a moment like a flower on his shirt pocket before it blew up and out of the truck.

"There'll be a frost tonight," Belle said. "Hog-killing weather, Pete calls it." She slowed the truck. "Ever been to Floyd's place?"

Rosa shook her head. She always felt uneasy about this stretch of road lined with black hemlocks. She wouldn't want to have a flat tire here where the dirt lane dips into the hollow. Belle swung to make the turn as if it were an unaccustomed gesture. The track angled down through the hemlocks where it was dark and bare of undergrowth. The cemetery must be there, but in the shadow Rosa could only see patches of light through the trunks. They came onto a field with a collection of weathered outbuildings and a trailer, its green paint oxidized, its windows covered with plastic. A brown hound pulled himself from a pile of straw in front of a shed and barked in a deep hoarse voice.

"Shut up, Bear," Belle said. "I'm bringing your friend home."

Buster bounced on Rosa's lap. As soon as she opened the door, he dropped to the floor, then onto the grass. The women watched the dogs twist and stretch in greeting.

Floyd was awake. He'd pulled off his cap and was sitting with his head down, his heels together, knees apart, rocking slightly as if from the momentum of a push. His hands were curled in his lap and his lids half-covered his eyes. Rosa could not remember what color they were, if she ever knew.

"What's the matter with you, Floyd Trask?" Belle leaned toward him. "You were plumb in the middle of the road. Do you want to get killed?"

He shook his head without looking up.

"What if someone else found you? You know where you'd be?"

He stopped rocking and raised his head to look at Belle.

"They can't put me in," he said. "Ain't no walls will hold me."

"It's up to you," Belle said. "You lay in the road, they'll put you in or put you under, one way or other."

"I can see through their walls." He glanced sideways at the slatted side of the truck. "You won't let them, will you, Belle?"

"We'll do what we can. Now you get yourself together, and I'll make coffee. Come on, Rosa."

Rosa followed her to the trailer through a scatter of hens picking about in the grass. Firewood, split into stove lengths, was stacked on an open porch. Several pairs of boots were lined up side by side, and pine branches were laid down as a doormat.

Belle paused with her hand on the door and listened.

"Here they come," she said.

Rosa could hear the distant whine of a siren.

"If it's Howard, we're all right; a new man could give us a hard time," Belle said.

The siren sounded closer then cut off sharply. It must have turned into the lane.

Belle was already moving back to the truck. "He's out again."

Floyd had fallen against the spare tire with his head back, his mouth open. Belle shook him, but he showed no sign of waking. She nodded to Rosa, and together they closed the tailgate.

A van burst into the clearing with a flash of white and red lights circling. It pulled up, and Howard and a young man got out. Belle squinted into the glare.

"Timmy Mellott," she said. "You old enough to be a volunteer?"

"Finished school in June," he said. He stood next to Howard with his weight on one foot and looked around at the trailer.

"Hi, Belle." Howard settled his visored cap to keep the sun from his eyes. His shirt was pulled tight across the mound of his belly, his pants buckled low with a wide belt. "Floyd's done it this time," he said.

"What do you mean?" Belle had her hands on her hips as if she could hide Floyd from their view.

"Some guy comes boiling into the rescue squad. Said he almost ran over Floyd laying in the road; claims he'd been hit."

"Well, he wasn't," Belle said. She turned suddenly toward the woods. "Did he follow you here?"

"Jeez. I didn't think of that," Howard said.

A dark green car, low slung and foreign made, came out of the woods. It moved slowly, pitching over the ruts. They watched it stop; a man got out on one side and slammed the door. He came toward them leaning into each step. The woman stayed with her hand resting on her open door.

"Well, where is he?" The man spoke to Howard.

Howard paused for a moment as if trying to think who the man was talking about. Then he shrugged his shoulders and looked toward Belle. She did not move.

"Well?" The man thrust his head forward; he glanced around at the trailer, the woodshed, the privy. Belle had her back to the truck, her legs slightly apart.

"Are you the woman who manhandled him into the truck?"

Belle looked over his head toward the ridge. Rosa realized Belle was not going to speak. She'd seen this same look come over her when Pete talked about cutting their big oaks.

"Well?" he said again and took a short step toward her.

Rosa waited another beat and then said, "Yes, we brought him home."

The man twisted around. "Oh." There was a slight drop in his voice as if he had checked a movement or changed what he was going to say.

"He's best off in his own home," Rosa said.

"Where is he now?" The man spoke to Howard again. "My wife says he was drunk. Filthy drunk, I'd say."

Rosa glanced at Belle and with the edge of her eye saw Floyd spread-eagled against the tire. There was no way to hide him if the man looked through the slats.

The woman by the car shifted her weight; she could see directly into the pickup's bed.

"Richard." The woman spoke quietly.

"I want to see him," the man said.

"Are you a physician?" Rosa asked. As soon as she said it, she knew it was a mistake. His expression didn't change, but he took on a deeper color, and when he spoke his voice was thick.

"He's an alcoholic and a derelict and needs help."

"Richard." The woman's voice was not loud, but insistent. He snapped his head toward her without looking at her.

"I'm handling this, Tina," he said.

She pushed her hands into her pockets and raised her shoulders. When he swung back to Howard, his stance shifted slightly away from the truck. No one said anything. Timmy leaned his elbow on the fender of the ambulance; Howard stared at the trailer. Their silence was like an arm pushing against the man's chest.

"This isn't the end," he said as he started toward his car. He opened the door and stood with it in front of him. "The authorities will hear of this. They'll hear about the conditions of this place." He was talking to Howard. "Come on, Tina. Get in."

Before she turned, the woman looked at Rosa and Belle without smiling, but to each one she nodded very slightly. Then, as if cold, she reversed the collar of her coat with her thumbs and held it closed with both hands before she ducked into the car.

They watched the car, sharp edged as a hawk's shadow, circle back to the woods. The sound of the motor faded, and Rosa heard the dogs scrabbling together, the click of Bear's collar.

"Jeez." Howard pulled a cigarette from a pack in his shirt pocket and brought out a wooden match. He scraped his thumbnail across the head to light it. Timmy opened the tailgate. Floyd was moving again.

"At least you kept your mouth shut," Belle said. "Now get out and get cleaned up."

Floyd rolled onto his hands and knees, his head hanging like a sick animal's. He lowered himself backward from the pickup. Timmy took his arm and led him to the trailer.

"Walk him round first," Belle said, "then clean him up."

Howard sat in the van filling out a form on a clipboard. Belle watched Timmy lead Floyd back of the trailer toward the stream.

A few days later, Rosa was sweeping leaves from the porch when Belle drove up with Buster and Bear in the truck bed. Bear's ears blew out flat in the wind. Belle stopped by the steps and spoke to Rosa through the open window.

"Did you hear about Floyd? Some Samaritan reported him laying out under the interstate bridge. The police come and took him off, shipped him to a center clear out in the western part of the state."

"I'm sorry, Belle," Rosa said. "Really sorry."

"Well," Belle looked in the direction of the barn and let out her breath. "Anyway, Buster here's got a friend," she said. "I'll have to freeze Floyd's hens before they start eating grain. His cats are so wild they'll take care of themselves."

"Is there anything we can do?"

Belle, still facing the barn, shook her head and touched her knuckles to her mouth. "At least he'll eat right. He'll be out come spring."

Rosa smoothed Bear's ears back with both her hands as if she had known him a long time.

"Rosa," Belle swung toward her. "I do believe you let go the old asparagus bed up behind the barn."

"I didn't know it was there," Rosa said.

"I'll show you." Belle climbed down from the truck.

"Bring a fork."

Rosa picked up a garden fork from the toolshed, and they walked down the slope to the barn. Belle angled off from the path opposite the raspberry beds and moved slowly through the tall yellowed grass. She pointed out dried skeletons of asparagus fern with berries small and round as ladybugs' shells.

"Here." Belle took the fork and pushed it at an angle into the earth beside the fern stems. A piece of turf came away on the tines. She bent over and folded back the sod exposing a flat corm the size of a plate with small nodules around the edges.

"That's the crown," she said. "You'll need to get rid of the weeds. Shake the soil out good and mulch it with manure. It'll come back to bearing."

As soon as Belle drove off, Rosa began forking the ground. She loosened weed roots from the deep-seated crowns and thought about this gift from Belle, but Belle had made a mistake. It was the woman, Tina, with the silk scarf who deserved the gift; she had thrust her hands under Floyd without wincing. Rosa remembered her own tight gestures, her quick glance at Belle, her chill of disdain for Tina watching from the verge.

Rosa leaned on her fork. Sun warmed her shoulders where she stood just outside the barn's shadow. A flight of migrating goldfinch fed among the grasses crossing and recrossing the line of shade. She pushed a strand of hair from her face and thought of Floyd sleeping with the jaunty yellow leaf caught on his shirt; she thought of Belle and Tina and herself bending together, raising him up onto the truck. Now she remembered—Floyd's eyes were blue, slate blue, the color of the ridges stretching west and south behind the barn.

High Water

"There'll be flooding," Stan said. He stood by the window in yellow foul-weather gear and watched rain sheet across the yard. Three days of downpour had followed the season's first blizzard, a thick heavy snow that in hours turned the tawny countryside black and white.

The girls were at breakfast; their brother, Alex, coming from the barn, stopped on the porch to stamp mud off his boots. When he entered the kitchen, he brought with him a circle of damp air.

"It's a river out there." He pushed wet hair off his forehead.

"This'll warm you." Cory held out a mug of coffee; Alex glanced at her and nodded as he took the cup.

"They'll be calling a flood alert." Stan did not turn from the window. "Keep the monitor on," he said.

"Like in a blizzard?" Amy said. She slid from the stool and went to collect her books and her coat.

"I always liked a storm," Cory said.

"A flood's different," Stan said, "tricky. It'll undercut where you can't see. A bridge might look sound, but a half ton of water can buckle it like an empty beer can."

"Where will you be?"

"Could be anywhere—river, canal, the bridge. I won't know until the dispatcher sends us."

"Eat up, kids, we'll be late," Alex said.

Stan swung around toward him. "Follow me to the road in that toy of yours." He caught Cory's glance. "I don't want her hauling you out of a rut."

Alex rinsed his mug at the sink. "I have four-wheel drive, remember?"

Cory picked a red-and-black hunting cap off the hook by the door and held it out to Stan. "You'll need this."

He unfolded the ear flaps. "And you take care, if you go

out. Hear?"

"You, too." She passed him his lunch box.

Cory watched them go through the forest of geraniums in the kitchen window, the garden window, she called it. Stan and Alex had built it for her for Christmas two years ago, and her plants flowered there all winter. The trucks jounced down the lane, Alex's little pickup first, Stan following close on his tail. Alex won't like that, Cory thought; she wondered whether Stan would pass him on the straight bit.

There was a time Stan rarely let Alex out of his sight. It was one of the things that first drew her to Stan, the way he cared for his son. The year Stan courted her, Alex was nine. Stan would take the two of them to the Thursday night cattle auction. He'd tell Cory what to look for in a sound heifer. She felt they were family, even then. Once at the county fair, she watched the two of them in a shooting gallery knock over row after row of moving ducks. They didn't stop until Stan missed a shot. Alex had given Cory the huge blue bear he won. After the babies came, Stan would watch Alex play with his sisters the way he'd watch the feeder calves, not smiling, holding quiet as if to keep pride at bay.

But recently something harsh had come between him and Alex. He couldn't let the boy be; they rarely worked together any more. Stan would send him out to the barn or into the fields on some project. When Cory tried to talk about Alex, Stan would turn to some chore, and she'd wonder if she had done something wrong.

The rain eased off by midday, and as Cory drove back from the Super Saver, the overcast began to break into loose cloud with a glint of harsh blue beyond. She checked the rearview mirror. The cartons of groceries were riding steady, and Rowdy, the black sheepdog, stood forefeet on the spare tire, his fur flattened by the wind. She snapped on the radio and caught the end of the weather report: high pressure, a cold front moving in. Then another voice, a National Weather Bureau bulletin, "A flood warning is in effect along the Potomac. Due to runoff of melting snow and rain, flooding is expected. Keep tuned to your local station for updates."

Their farm lay three miles from the river; the kids would be safe at home by now. From the cut on Town Ridge, Cory saw an unaccustomed brightness in the valley where the river had spread. At the fork, Cory turned onto the road that passed through town; it was only minutes longer, and she wanted to see the flood up close. The lower end of Main Street was clogged with traffic as she edged past cars and pickups double parked. People were loading them with boxes, TVs, armfuls of clothes. The Ford dealer's lot was empty, and at Ace Lumber, Marlis was shifting plywood with a forklift onto a flatbed. He waved as her truck rumbled over the train tracks toward the river.

Cory drove across the canal to the parking lot by the town's boat ramp, and with the engine still running, walked to the grass bank above the river. Rowdy jumped down to sniff the edge of water that pushed up the tarmac in small leaps and jerks. On the far side, the river pressed deep into the trees, and close by it pulled the underbrush in strange, bobbing rhythms. Branches, beer cans, and foam coiled in the back eddy where a culvert spilled a clay-colored stream into the river. The two currents met in a choppy roil, one side brown, the other red. The air smelled of cold earth, like the entrance to a cave.

Rowdy, ears forward, neck curved, pawed the flotsam, lifting his foot above a circle of tiny waves that vibrated as if a bee were caught in the drift. The small thrashing came from a twist of red—a salamander searching for security on a floating stick. Cory squatted down and slipped her hand under it. It lay still, ribs beating like a watch tick through translucent orange skin. She closed her fingers over it and carried it to where the slope leveled off at the towpath, and there, let the salamander slide free. For a moment, it paused before starting off in little half swings, four-toed feet splayed on the wet ground. It's safe, she told herself as she walked back to the truck, but knew it might not be so.

The unpaved road followed the canal for a bit then turned up through the orchards. The school bus had already passed. Buddy Krupshaw was riding his bicycle through puddles in front of his family's blue trailer. The kids would be in the kitchen, Alex setting out a snack. He had taken to doing this when they got home from school, then he'd see they started their homework before he began on the barn chores. Alex was good with his sisters—his stepsisters, her stepson.

Cory didn't think of him that way. He was part of life with Stan. When she first moved into the house, Stan and Alex weren't used to anyone else around. At meals they didn't say much, and sometimes Cory felt her voice was breaking through mist. It was as if she had to teach them to talk together. Alone with her, each one was easier. Stan wasn't exactly talkative, but they'd sit at the table after dinner; she'd tell him about a new litter of barn cats or what Minna Deneen said at the church's Sisterhood meeting. He'd watch her and smile, would sometimes have a story about the road crew.

The first summer, Alex had showed her around the place. Although she'd grown up in the next valley, her father worked for the phone company, and she knew little about farms. Alex taught her how to put a halter on a calf, how to break open a bale of hay and shake out the square clumps, *books* he called them. Sometimes she'd make sandwiches, and she and Alex would go to the river to swim or fish. One Sunday, she got Stan to borrow a boat and take them out on the river. She and Alex had often spoken about exploring the little islands they could see from the bank, but Stan didn't want to land, said the mosquitoes would get them. He rowed them to a place where he claimed the fish lay and anchored there. Every time someone moved and the boat rocked a bit, he'd reach his hand toward Alex. Later he told Cory he had never learned to swim.

After Elsa was born, there was no time for fishing, but she and Alex still had quiet talks when they weeded the garden together or sat on the porch paring apples. Once they watched a skein of geese stream out of an autumn fog and fly low across the pasture, voices trailing long after the blank sky had taken them back.

"How do they know the way?" Alex had asked.

"Some part of them knows," she said. "Instinct, like a foal knows its mother."

He had looked into the white distance without speaking. Cory heard her own words and wanted to hug him.

As she swung into their lane, Cory could see Alex's truck in front of the house, the kids sitting on the porch steps, and Alex leaning in shadow against the wall. He stepped forward as she drove up.

"Pop phoned," Elsa said. "He's working overtime."

"They're closing River Road."

"But it's way above the water, I was just there."

"There's a thirty-five-foot crest expected," Alex said. "They've called out the National Guard and asked the high school seniors to volunteer. Lenore Stutz needs you to help at the church canteen. Gran said she'd take the kids."

"Can we go, Ma? We're ready." Elsa held up a bundle of clothes.

"I'll drive them over," Alex said. All three watched her face.

"First we unload."

Alex opened the tailgate and carried the cartons into the kitchen. Elsa handed her mother the frozen food to pack in the freezer; Amy folded the bags.

"The stock needs feeding," Cory said.

"I've already done it, and shut in the hens with water and grain."

"Take sweaters. It's going to turn cold."

"We can go!" Amy went for their pullovers.

"You can go." Cory buttoned the top of Elsa's jacket. "Come right back, Alex. I'll call Gran that you're on your way."

"Twenty minutes," Alex said. He closed the door on the girls' side and pressed the lock.

In the kitchen, the CB monitor crackled out a call for a rescue crew to evacuate an elderly couple from a trailer by the canal. Cory took a stack of pies from the freezer and set them in a basket then phoned her mother, but the line was busy. When she went to get her boots from the closet, she found them already set in the hall along with flashlights, a Coleman lantern, and a can of fuel.

Stan didn't see Alex the way she did. Nowadays around his father, the boy closed off. They seemed to have lost connection. Sometimes Cory thought Stan would rather have Alex hanging out in the A & P parking lot on Saturday night drinking illegal beer with his classmates than have him work on his truck with his friend Donald. In the past year, the little imported pickup had taken most of Alex's spare time. He'd bought it from the Texaco station after it was hauled off the interstate as totaled. He and Donald spent most of last year rebuilding it. They haunted salvage yards to find parts and only last month painted it black and put an orange stripe around it with blue-edged flames on the fenders.

Cory thought Stan would be pleased, but even the truck got his goat. Once he called it a Japanese doll's car. Alex claimed Stan was sore because it was the only decent looking vehicle on the place. "A faggot truck," Stan said. Alex spun around as if Stan had slapped him; he'd slammed the door and driven off. His father watched him go, then shut his eyes tight as if with a wince of pain.

It had been some time since Cory had talked with Alex of anything beyond daily events. She missed him. But recently he'd given her a new kind of attention, had taken to doing small things. Without her asking, he whitewashed the stone smokehouse where she kept the garden tools. Then at dinner a few weeks ago, he had said, "Cory has a new sweater." It was one she'd found at the Goodwill store, pale green and fine soft wool. Made in Scotland, the label said. Everyone had stopped eating and looked, not at Cory, but at Alex. She rose to clear the table. "Thank you," she said. Alex had mopped his plate with bread.

Stan started in about Alex signing up with the navy. The recruiting office had sent a letter saying his test scores indicated Alex had the aptitudes they were looking for. Alex planned to go to the community college and had lined up a job at the Texaco station working nights and weekends; his father claimed the navy would educate him free.

Stan had been with the Seabees in Korea and had learned to handle heavy equipment there. When he came home, he got a job with the Road Commission that he's had ever since. Although he didn't talk much about the navy, whenever it was mentioned, he'd speak carefully as if he didn't want to boast or give away a secret. It was a part of his life, separate and private, like his first marriage, and Cory did not belong there.

One evening after the girls were in bed and Alex gone off to his room, Stan didn't turn on the TV, but stayed at the kitchen table.

"More coffee?" Cory held out the blue pot.

"Sure." He watched his mug fill.

"Here." Cory set a pitcher of milk on the table and sat down across from him.

It felt good to have him there again, just the two of them. Stan stirred his coffee. She knew he wanted to speak about Alex.

"He works hard, Stan," Cory said, "gets good marks."

"And fools around with that car and that kid, Donald."

"They made it run, made it real pretty."

"Pretty," he pressed a crumb against the tablecloth.

"He wants to go to college."

"The navy'd teach him a trade."

"Is that what troubles you?"

Stan looked up. "What do you mean?"

"Is that what matters, a trade?"

"The farm won't make him a living; he's got to have a trade."

"He can learn a trade in college."

"That's not it. He's got to get out of here. Get away."

"The navy's rough."

"Maybe he needs rough."

Cory shook her head. "What he needs is for you to see him."

"I see him all right. I see the two of them bent under the hood of that damned truck."

"Donald's his friend. In college he'd meet other people, all sorts of people."

"It's like we're talking about different things." Stan stood up and walked to the window and ran a finger across a geranium leaf.

Cory carried the boots and basket onto the porch. Alex was back, setting a coil of rope in his truck bed.

"We're taking yours?"

"I have a spotlight. We may need it." Alex paused with his hand on the fender.

"Right," she said.

He called Rowdy and clipped the dog to his chain. Cory taped a note for Stan on the door. "He might stop in and wonder where we are," she said.

Alex shrugged and started the engine. He steered straddling the ruts with the same precise assurance of his father. What had come between them? Was it anything she had done? A distant stretch of the river lay flat and silver, filling the valley floor. At the intersection with the county road, Wayne Hyler in a Day-Glo vest waved them down. He wore a field phone and a flashlight strapped to his belt.

Alex rolled the window open and Wayne leaned down. "We're only letting essential traffic through."

"They called the high school seniors to volunteer," Alex said. "Cory's helping at the canteen."

Cory bent forward. "Can you get Stan on that phone?"

"I can get the dispatcher at Commission headquarters."

"Could you have him tell Stan I'm at the church and Alex is at the school?"

"Sure." Wayne slapped their fender. "See you for coffee break." He waved them on.

"You shouldn't have bothered," Alex said. "He doesn't give a damn where we are."

"You're wrong. He worries all the time."

She knew Alex didn't believe her and let his silence be. They passed a military truck on the edge of town.

"What'll you be doing?" Cory asked.

"They'll assign us at school. Donald's waiting so we can work together."

Donald was a nice boy, mannerly, the only friend Alex ever brought home. His family had moved from the city two years ago, and since then he and Alex spent their free time together. Donald has a way with motors. Stan even let him tune the trucks, but he didn't like his being around. Cory was relieved that Alex had a friend. Like his father, Alex was a loner, shy. She tried to make it easier for them, but sometimes she felt they both expected something of her that she couldn't give.

Alex pulled up by the church.

"Here, take this." Cory held out a packet of brownies.

Alex looked at her hand and hesitated. "Thanks."

She closed the door with her elbow. "I'll look for you later."

The church kitchen was bright and steamy. Cory realized it was getting dark outside. Lenore Stutz turned from peeling an onion. "Cory, I just said you'd be here. Didn't I, girls? Grab an apron."

Cory tied a wide flowered apron over her jeans.

"We're doing spaghetti to serve here, hamburgers to send out. Then cole slaw and pie," Lenore told her. "Your turn with the onions. I'm bawling like a baby."

Cory laughed and took her place by the sink.

The hall began to fill with evacuees: old people, kids, mothers lugging plastic bags of clothes and toys. With paper tablecloths and the parish women in cheerful aprons, the place had the air of a church supper, as if the events outside were happening somewhere else. Then Elsie Hyler came in and reported the bridge fifteen miles upstream had gone. Traffic was still crossing here, but the Guard was turning back heavy trucks. Water was up to the towpath. Cory thought of the salamander; she'd been wrong.

Old Lloyd Moser held forth at the end of a table with stories of the '34 flood. "The river come up so fast, two men got caught in their barn. Climbed onto the roof, but the whole thing went. Never found one of them."

A bus arrived to transfer evacuees to the school where they had set up beds, but then a bunch of high school kids came in talking and joshing. They had loaded the picnic tables from the park and moved them up behind the A & P. Cory set a platter of spaghetti at their table and asked if anyone had seen Alex.

"He went to round up Hassler's steers. The pasture's bottomland with no high ground."

Cory knew the Hassler farm, a pretty stone house set back from the road close to a creek with hemlocks around it. The fields stretched along a narrow valley that widened where the stream emptied into the river. The cattle wintered in the far pasture. It had a windbreak of trees and a hay barn with a feeding shed attached. To get to it, you crossed the stream by a plank bridge.

Wayne Hyler came in for coffee. He said two trailers and a fishing cabin had washed away. Cory wrapped hamburgers and passed them on to Minna Deneen who was making up carryout lunches. The road crew was sandbagging the railroad bridge, Wayne said. Cory thought of Stan in the glass cab of a front-end loader; he'd lean to watch the bucket, hands working the gears with the certainty of an artist.

The hall began to empty out. The high school kids left with Marlis when he came by looking for volunteers to shift lumber.

"Let's take a break." Lenore wiped her hands on her apron. Minna set out plastic cups; Elsie put down half a layer cake.

Cory carried her coffee outside to the parking lot and stood behind a group of men listening to a monitor in one of the trucks. At Little Orleans, the water rose fifteen feet in twenty minutes; the river would crest here in about an hour. None of the men had seen Alex.

In the cemetery behind the church, it was dark enough to make out the Big Dipper over Town Ridge. Cory could see headlights move slowly across the bridge, but not the growing river. It was there, hissing against trees and carrying inside it broken fences, houses, books, picture albums, toys. As she started back, a yellow highway truck pulled fast into the church parking lot. Stan jumped down and headed for the kitchen.

Cory ran after him. "Stan." She touched his arm. "You OK?"

He swung around fast. "Where's Alex?" The bones of his face stood out sharp in the overhead light.

"They say he went to Hassler's farm a while ago."

"No one's seen his truck at either end of town. I'm going to find him."

"Hold a minute. I'll get my boots."

When she came out, Stan had turned the pickup; he started off before she could close the door.

"We'll cut through Brightly's orchard and come out above Hassler's. The road's underwater where the stream crosses. Hang on. It'll be rough."

The hill shut out the lights of the town, but a pink glow showed behind the bare apple trees. Cory put her hands on the dashboard to steady herself as the truck bucked between the rows. The headlights caught on tussocks of grass throwing jagged shadows on the uneven ground. When they reached the tarmac, its blackness seemed smooth and empty, then a red reflector gleamed at the entrance to the Hassler farm. May stood beside their old Pontiac; Gene sat in the cab of the farm truck with its door open; the back was piled with boxes and loose clothes. An aluminum boat tilted on the grass. Stan pulled even with the car.

"Hey there, Gene, May."

"We're watching it go." Gene said, "Nothing more we can do."

"He crossed three times in the boat, then switched off the gas and come to watch," May added.

"It'll be halfway up the kitchen now. The current's too strong to cross even with someone hauling a rope."

"He didn't get the cat," May said.

"Have you seen Alex?"

The question came out harsh and loud.

"Earlier. He was by earlier," Gene said, "with another kid. Said they'd cut the fence and turn the steers into the woods up behind the pasture."

"Did he come back?"

"Didn't notice," May said. "It was a good half hour ago."

"I'll check," Stan said.

"There's water in the dip. It's backing up fast now. Don't be long."

A quarter mile down the road, their lights caught a strip of water slick as black ice across the road.

"Jesus," Stan's voice was tight as if he were angry.

Cory held onto the seat even though it was smooth riding. Their wheels splashed through the water, throwing out an arc of water. As Stan swung through the pasture gate, the headlights picked out Alex's truck a few feet from where water edged over the grass.

Stan jumped out and stood at the edge of the water calling Alex's name. He didn't wait for an answer but opened the door of the little pickup. "Where the hell's the switch?" He fumbled on the dashboard.

"Here." Cory was beside him.

The spotlight went on sharp as a gunshot. Trees rose silver from black water, pocked and streaked where the current swirled. Stan swept the beam along the edge of trees. Suddenly a cluster of amber points shone from the woods.

"Cattle." Stan's voice was low, almost a whisper.

He pressed the horn, three short blasts. The swinging light caught the side of the barn, a bright flat surface, then, half-hidden in shadow, the shed. Someone stood on the roof waving and shouting although Cory couldn't hear the words over the sound of the river.

"It's Alex," Stan said.

"How can you tell?" Cory could make out only a moving figure.

"It's Alex."

"And Donald?"

"Take the truck," Stan said. "Get Gene's boat."

Cory ran to the pickup.

"Don't cross the dip too fast, you'll wet the distributor."

She was hardly aware of driving or what she said, but they loaded the boat into the pickup; May lay the oars alongside it. Cory sat in the bed holding the boat steady; Gene took the wheel. He broke through the dip without slowing, spraying wide white wings. Then they were back. Together he and Stan set the boat in the water.

"We need rope," Stan said.

Cory lifted the coil from Alex's truck and handed it to him. He looped the carefully whipped end through a ring on the boat, his fingers working fast. He tested the knot then climbed to the center seat and set the oars. Gene pushed the boat into the black river and began to play out rope as Stan rowed upstream in rough jerks.

"Stan can't swim."

"He'll manage," Gene said. "Stan has luck. Look how he found you."

The current caught and drew the boat suddenly sideways. Gene braced; Cory grabbed the line behind him. Her shoulders tightened, the rope twisted in her hand; she felt the river's thrum and the jolt as Stan fought against the current. They played out more line, until suddenly it sagged slack. Above the sound of the river and her heaving breath, Cory heard a metallic bang and voices.

The light began to die.

"Better start the motor, the lamp's drawing down the battery," Gene said. "And take it up the hill a piece."

Water was already lapping at the front tires. When Cory started the engine, the light brightened. She backed up the slope and refocused the spot, but even then she could only dimly make out two figures moving on the roof. They leaned down and seemed to lift something.

"They got the boy there," Gene said.

"Which boy?"

"Can't no way tell."

The sound of a shout reached them, and hand over hand, she and Gene started to haul in wet rope. Cory could make out Stan's back as he stretched and drew against the oars. The figure in the stern was bent over, but she recognized Alex's blue sweatshirt. Even when the boat slid onto the ground, he didn't look up. Stan stepped out of the boat and pulled its front end onto the grass.

"Get him in the truck," he said.

"We got to keep his leg straight," Alex said. He stood up. "Cory, there's a blanket in the cab."

She found an old quilt folded on the seat. Alex laid the oars on the ground with the quilt under them, then lashed the rope to hold it in place. Gene knelt beside Donald on the floor of the boat.

"He ain't talking," he said, "but he's breathing."

"Shock," Alex said. "We got to get him warm."

He had already covered Donald's body with his jacket. Cory rummaged in the back of Stan's highway truck for a tarp. The three men lifted Donald onto the makeshift stretcher and into the truck bed. Cory climbed in beside him and laid the tarp over him.

"Better get the boat," Stan said.

Alex stepped from the circle of light to the far side of the boat. He held himself stiff, alert, as if waiting. Behind him the river hissed and churned. He's safe, Cory thought, but she was aware of another force, as if a feeder stream, heavy with earth, had entered the current. She was only a witness and could change nothing between them.

Stan turned slowly toward his son; he put his hand on the boat's side opposite Alex. They looked at each other then, feet gripping the sodden ground, leaned their weight forward and together pulled the boat clear of the water, sliding it along the slope. They drew the boat higher and higher as if it had no weight at all, as if it were a great joy to drag the awkward hull up the pasture hill against the pull of gravity.

Magnus Isn't Here

Dan carried the chain saw down to the pickup with Magnus trotting beside him as if on a close heel; the dog's sleek, black back grazed Dan's left hand. After he hefted the saw into the truck bed, Dan climbed in the cab and slammed the door without turning around. The dog whined, and, rearing onto his hind feet, planted his forepaws on the door. "Down!" Dan pushed the star on his chest, and Magnus dropped, squatting on his haunches, his thin tail brushing the dirt.

"Call him, will you?" Dan yelled. "I have to get off."

I clapped my hand on my thigh. "Magnus. Here boy." The dog paid no attention. I walked over and put my hand under his collar.

"Stay." Dan started the engine. I had to pull Magnus's resisting body toward me. He twisted away; the chain pinched my fingers, and with a surge of anger I yanked at the collar hard, feeling his weight in my fingers. Magnus yelped but never shifted his eyes from the truck. Only when it disappeared into the dip below the house did he quit fussing and come along with me onto the terrace where he lay with his head pointed toward the road.

In the kitchen, I poured myself fresh coffee and looked out at the unhampered space stretching across the sage flats to the mesas and beyond to mountains mounded with cumulus. Even after five years, the view still startles me, but this morning I had to clean an image of Dan's stony face from my mind before I connected with the casual sweep of land. I pulled the thought of this small interruption from me like a burr from my skin.

When he came East for our wedding, Dan said he learned a lot about me from seeing the New England village where I'd grown up. At the time I was pleased, but later wondered if he felt stifled by the braided hills and restricted sky. Here in this wide land, I am alert to shifting light, the smell of dust and juniper, or a flick of movement at the edge of my eye, although if I turn my head, usually I find everything is still.

I carried my coffee onto the terrace and knew, before I saw the imprint where he had lain on the dusty tiles, that Magnus had gone. On the flats below, a wake of dust drifted behind the pickup. It's a mile to the road, but in the clear air, the shadow of the truck was sharper than the truck itself. Magnus broke from the scrub on the far side of the dip stretching in wide leaps, closing the distance to the moving pickup. He might catch it before the blacktop, but Dan wouldn't see him. Magnus leaned into the curve before the last straight run. I shouted and waved, but it was hopeless, and Dan wouldn't look back at me.

He would have rolled the windows open; air would flow through the cab as the faded red fenders sliced past mesquite and sage. In the side mirror the dog, running head down, his pale yellow eyes wide, would rise and fall with each bound. If Dan caught a gleam of the reflected leap in the circle of receding mesquite, the cab would fill with heat, and anger would burst like a bullet through the window tracing its fine arc to me.

I started running. Once on the valley road, Dan, late already, would gun the truck and outdistance the dog. Magnus wouldn't stop. I swung into the gully where dun-colored earth and twisted live oaks cut off the view of the flats. The sound of my feet was muted; my body eased into long strides, arms and shoulders swinging in counter rhythm, my breath ample. At the bottom of the dip, I crossed a pool of night air. Had Magnus felt this cool drift? Did he delight in running? When I came out on the lower slope, both truck and dog were gone. Perhaps he had given up and flopped by the road in a low shadow, his black sides heaving, his tongue quivering with each breath. I slowed to a walk, aware of stones hot under my bare feet. It was dumb to go on, but I had to make amends for the chain biting into the dog's neck.

Magnus belongs to Dan. Dan got him two years ago when I went home for a visit after a miscarriage. It was a hard visit. My father's medical colleagues had confirmed

Doc Tucker's opinion that a successful pregnancy was un-
likely. After the report, I stayed on with my parents for a few
weeks, thinking the familiar countryside might somehow
absorb the terrifying emptiness that had opened around me.
But the soft hills seemed closed in, the summer woods too
lush, and my mother's unspoken compassion, stifling. I
ached for harsh dry sky and space.

Dan met my plane. He was waiting by the gate in his
faded jeans, and when he saw me, lifted his arm over his
head high, as if I were a long way off. I was carrying a coat
and bag and did not wave in answer. Crossing the apron, I
winced against the desert sun, against the sudden loosening
within me. Dan leaned across the barrier, his dark eyes wide,
as if they failed to narrow to protect him from the blast of
light. He'd put his arm around me, but I couldn't bear to join
our pain; my tears drew back, and I was tight with shame at
what I failed to do. We talked about my parents and the
ranch as we walked to the truck.

Magnus, a half-grown pup at the time, was tied in back.
He greeted Dan as if he were the one who had been away for
a month.

"What do you think?" Dan rumpled the dog's ears.

I held my hand out, but he twisted to lick Dan's fingers.

"He has yellow eyes," I said.

Dan taught Magnus to sit and lie; he'd wait in one spot
for hours until a signal would release him in a trajectory to
Dan. Sometimes he would mind what I said, but only after a
glance at Dan's face; alone with me, he'd cringe as if afraid
I'd strike him. Dan claims he was maltreated as a pup, but I
think Magnus is crazy. His parents were supposed to be aris-
tocratic Great Danes, but it seems his mother had run with a
local dog, perhaps even a coyote. In any case, his lines are
handsome: sleek black, solid muscle under the skin, and
strange pale eyes, and like a dog in a Bruegel painting, his
bone-thin tail hangs low.

When Dan goes to check fences or count cattle, Magnus
is always with him. I used to ride out with Dan on the grey
filly he gave me as a wedding present; we'd lope alongside
each other, weaving through the sage, Dan leading with his
big bay. At midday, we'd tether the horses and lie under a
pinon to eat our sandwiches. Occasionally we'd make love

on the rough ground with only our shirts to lie on. It's been some time now since I rode with Dan.

A few weeks ago, Dan came home with a calf across his saddle and a cow following. He'd seen buzzards circling low and figured there was a dead animal in the arroyo, he said. The dog, ranging the brush, found a cow straining to give birth, and he'd barked until Dan came. "She was in trouble. I had to push the calf back and turn it so it could be born," Dan said. "We would have lost them both, cow and calf, but Magnus beat out those old buzzards." As he spoke, Dan had stroked the dog's head. I remember the movement of his hand as sharply as if he had touched my hair.

He used to take Magnus to town with him, but a few months ago he decided the dog should stay on the ranch. I'd hold him until the truck was gone; then Magnus would sit on the terrace, and sometimes he'd let out a fine high howl that stretched like a kite string into the dry air.

Crossing the flats, I watched, not my feet, but the ground in front, choosing patches free from stones. Later, Dan would say, "Why did you let him go?" I didn't let him go. Or did I? Sometimes I wonder if I contrive to make happen the things he blames on me.

The dirt track rose sharply to the blacktop, and the smell of tar mixed with dust and sage. I crossed the hot rails of the cattle guard and touched the tarmac with my foot. I wouldn't walk the two miles to the next ranch, but I came this far. I would tell Dan. I came this far.

Shadows had gone from the hills, and shapes flattened in the direct light. As I turned back, I could hardly distinguish the adobe house and my workshop from the slope behind; only the barn roof glinted in the sun. I'm an early riser and had been up since five. In the first years of our marriage, Dan used to reach out when I'd stir in bed and touch me as if to hold me in the hammock of sleep. At breakfast he'd call me Worthy Puritan.

This morning, I'd lain on my back watching faint light streak the ceiling and listened to Dan breathe beside me. It was Thursday, his day to go to town. I considered waking him but figured to let him lie in, not because he was unwilling to wake, but my habit of rising early makes him uneasy, like a silent reproach. He'd spend the day trying to even the righteousness score. I wondered if this touchiness was something I'd taught him.

When I first met Dan, the year I transferred to Colorado, he seemed as clear and open as the land itself. But sage flats, I'd found, can be cut by hidden arroyos you don't see until you're right on top of them. The first time Dan took me to the far end of our section, we rode through scattered pine, and suddenly he reined up on the rim of a canyon. Below us a stream flowed through bright grass under a stand of cottonwoods. We'd left the horses and climbed down, following the stream to a pool where a twist of water sluiced from a cliff. We'd stripped and swum together in the stunning water.

The terrace was still dark when I went out this morning. Magnus had padded over and stretched his front feet, arching his back, yawning. Since Dan took to leaving him, he's become more tolerant of me and sometimes lies in my studio doorway facing the road. I suspect it's a better lookout place than the terrace. When Dan's in the house, Magnus does not follow me.

The short walk to my workshop was like crossing a border. The same few stars were scattered over the black line of mountains, and the land continued to brighten, but it's another country there. I opened the door and switched on the track lamps over the cutting table. The room took shape. Bolts of cloth stood in wooden bins, scissors hung in diminishing sizes on the wall, drawings and measurements were pinned to a bulletin board. I like starting the day in this quiet order and doing an hour's work in the cool before breakfast.

Dan built the studio our second year on the ranch. We worked together laying adobe brick, setting the roof beams. It was a gift from Dan, the time he took. I finished plastering the interior myself, but he made the door for me. It's a beautiful door. He'd found some old planks weathered silver and had spent evenings fashioning geometric panels that radiate from a sunburst at the center. I helped him hang it, and afterward we sat on the steps drinking a beer to celebrate. The door caught the evening light reflecting it inward, brightening the whole room.

I design dresses for a shop on the plaza. It's a satisfactory business, and together with the cattle, we make a decent living on the ranch. I was working on an order for shirts in

Mexican cotton and had spread a length of bright green cloth on the table. I flattened the folds, stroking the rough grain with my palm. As I cut and pinned, my thoughts would dart to Dan, some word or gesture, as if trying to catch something I was not quick enough to see. I worked until the sun sloped through the open door. A lizard flicked across the scraps on the floor, pausing in the slit of sunlight, twisting its head from side to side. By straightening its front legs, the lizard raised its head an inch higher, widening its view to see a sign of danger or possible quarry from another angle. Something, the quiver of a fly, a bird's shadow, roused the lizard, and it skittered across the threshold out of sight. I stared at the empty bar of sunlight. If I shifted my line of vision, everything would change. Places I thought were connected could turn out to be separate; maybe the distant mountains are only foothills of further ranges.

When I returned to the house, Dan was making the bed. I went to the other side to help.

"It's OK," he said. "I've done it."

"How did you sleep?" I asked because he had been sleeping badly.

"Fine," he said.

"You didn't hear me get up?"

"No. I woke on my own time." He twitched the coverlet straight. "Toast and eggs are waiting."

The table was set, the eggs in a pan far too large did not have enough water to cover them. I lifted one out with a spoon and broke it open. It dripped like an icicle into the cup.

"Underdone for you?" Dan asked.

"Yes. You take it; it's how you like it."

Dan poured the coffee. "Have it while it's hot," he said.

We ate looking out at the dry hills.

"A lot to do in town?"

"Your list for Safeway."

"Are you meeting Harry?"

"Not enough time," Dan said. He pulled a paper from his shirt pocket. "Cattle feed, fan belt, lumber for your shelves. Anything for the shop?"

"No, I'll have an order ready next week."

"The chain saw needs a new blade."

"Back around five?"

"Later." Dan got up and set his cup in the sink. "There's four hours driving; these errands take time."

"Six-thirty then?"

"Hell, I don't know. I'll be here when I turn up."

"OK, OK. When you turn up, I'll have dinner ready."

He snatched the keys from the hook by the door, and I watched him down the steps.

"Don't forget the chain saw."

"Where is it?"

"By the door where you left it."

He came back for it without looking up.

"Good-bye," I said.

The climb back to the house was steep. My legs ached; heat radiating from the ground burned the soles of my feet. In the gully, I stopped and leaned over, breathing hard. It was still cool there; a horned toad crossed the ruts leaving a reticulated pattern in the dust. I straightened up and shouted for Magnus down the arroyo, but the earth walls absorbed my voice. I would tell Dan how I called and called.

On the terrace, I rinsed my feet in a bucket under the spigot, washing off the dust, cooling my blistered skin. Sometimes Magnus would drink here. I thought of him hunched over the bucket, his body jerking with each lap of his tongue, and like a sudden rip of cloth, I knew what Dan felt for him. At the same time, I knew my running was a sham. I wanted Magnus gone; I wanted Dan back, but I didn't have the dog's welcome to offer him. Instead I had shut his gleaming door and holed up in my studio. Water dried on my skin with a fine prickle; air stirred across my face and under my hair.

I caught movement in the valley. A pickup turned into our road, the Minot's blue Chevy. Maybe Becky had found Magnus. She's our neighbor, and she's taught me a lot about living alone the way we do. Her husband, Ted, helped us through the first rough years on the ranch. Dan's courses in ranch management and animal husbandry didn't seem to match reality. After my trip East, I told Becky I couldn't have a child. It had been eating at me, and I wanted to say it to someone. She was quiet for a long time. "I can't know how you feel, but fear of losing one of ours is always there along-

69

side me like a coyote running in the underbrush. Tending the kids lets me put off thinking about it, but bone deep I know he's running in the shadows." She touched my arm. "You have no buffer, Sarah. I'm sorry." I didn't like remembering what she said. It made me want to cry, but I wasn't able to.

The pickup came out of the gully fast, bucking over the cattle guard. It was Ted. He pulled up in front of the house and got out. A big man, but he moved easily, only a little stiff in one hip since he was thrown a couple of years ago.

"Hi there, young lady."

"Hi, Ted. I thought it was Becky."

"She went to Denver yesterday to see her sister."

"Dan's gone, too."

"Shipping cattle?"

"No. Prices are terrible. He's not selling."

"Me, either," he said.

"Ted, you didn't see Magnus on the road, did you?"

"Only Acey Blodgett. She passed by driving that van of hers hell-bent toward Mesa."

"I've lost Magnus."

"What do you mean, lost him? He'll be back."

"No. He took off after Dan this morning, running his heart out. He'll never catch up, and he won't stop."

"No animal's that dumb."

"Magnus is. He's loco. He gets frantic every time Dan leaves. Moons about, butts his head under my arm when I'm working. Drives me nuts."

"He'll turn up."

"Dan will be sore. He says I don't like Magnus."

"Ah, it's not serious," Ted looked toward the barn. "I came to borrow Dan's winch. Mine's jammed, and I'm fixing the bridge that washed out last storm."

"It's in the barn," I rubbed my hands on my jeans. "Would you be going to Mesa for the mail?"

Ted looked at me. "I could," he said.

"Would it be trouble to go there and back? The fan belt on the Dodge is broken."

He glanced at his watch. "For you, kid, no trouble." I knew he had a full day planned; he's a hard worker.

"Great. I'll get my shoes. I ran down to the road barefoot trying to catch that damned dog."

Ted shook his head and walked off to the barn.

In the house, I slipped on a pair of sandals and picked up my shoulder bag. As I passed through the kitchen, I took a Coke and a can of beer from the refrigerator. Ted already had the winch in the truck. He opened the door for me and went around to the other side.

The cab was cool but stuffy, the windows closed.

"Here." I held out a beer. "I brought you this."

My voice sounded odd, flat. Ted peeled off the tab and raised the can toward me before he leaned back for a long pull. "I'd do it without the beer," he said.

The air conditioner came on with the motor, and almost at once I felt cold.

"The last I saw of him was when I ran in here into the draw," I said. "He was headed for the main road."

"And you barefoot. Crazy Sarah."

The Coke was too sweet; its fizz was solid in my throat. I leaned forward scanning the flats. Nothing moved. Even the steers grazing by the north fence were still. But five, maybe six miles further on, a blur of movement threaded through squat shadows, the quiet broken by scattered stones and claws scoring the earth. Was it Dan's image or the smell of his hand or the hope for something more, some unknown want, that drove Magnus in that harsh rhythm?

"I envy that dog," I said. "He doesn't wonder why he does things."

"Seems you don't, either, running barefoot after him."

On the hardtop, we moved along fast, the straight road dipping and rising above itself narrower and further off until it disappeared in the shimmer below the mountains. Ted said Becky wanted him to build her an office. She does the books and a good deal of planning on their ranch. After my workshop was finished, Becky came over to see it; she didn't say much but touched the cupboard doors and ran her finger along the bins.

"Will you do it?"

"I guess, once I get the new cattle tank in and the bridge repaired."

"She'd like it."

"She keeps after me. An office, she says." He smiled. "It was right about here Acey practically ran me off the road;

she's a wild one, that."

"Maybe she's lonely," I said.

Acey stopped by the ranch a couple of days ago with some stuff for Dan about a cattle-feed supplement. He was off fixing a break in the fence, so we had coffee in the kitchen. She kept looking out the window as if she was in a hurry. I told her she could leave the stuff, but she said, no, she'd wait. Maybe she'd had a fight with her husband, Pete; I'd heard them argue often enough. Who knows?

Ahead of us, a car crossed the flats at right angles on the main highway. At the stop sign, an arrow pointed left—Albuquerque 109 Miles. We swung right and passed another sign—Mesa: Population 109. The coincidence always pleased Dan; he'd remark on it when we drove by. Ted pulled up in front of the general store and post office; across the street was a bar, a gas station, and a couple of houses.

"I'll ask Mrs. Purdy," I said.

"And get our mail if there is any," Ted said. "I'm going to fill up while we're here."

A double-paneled screen door to the store opened out from the middle; its wire spring was tight and slammed after me. The dark inside was lit by a single lightbulb in the post office cage where Mrs. Purdy was sorting mail. Her hair was tightly waved, and her harlequin glasses were flecked with gold.

"Hi, Mrs. Purdy. Any mail?"

"A magazine come. Dan was in earlier."

"Did you notice a dog? His black dog, Magnus?"

"Nope. No dog come in here. Want your magazine?"

"Please. Anything for the Minot's?"

"Nope." She handed me the magazine without looking up. "He was in same time as Acey Blodgett. Seems it's Thursday."

"Oh," I said. "Thursday." It took a long time for the sound of the words to reach my ears. I could hardly lift my arm; my fingers, thick and weighted, reached for the brown envelope.

"Thanks," I said to hear my voice. I accepted the magazine and turned toward the door. At the end of the aisle, the four panels of white light forced me to focus. I walked past dim shelves of folded work shirts and socks, leather laces on a card, bottles of aspirin. Light increased; the ceiling diffused in blackness. I could not see my hand on the panel of the door. Outside, I narrowed my eyes against the sun. I wanted to pull my arms over my face.

In the shadow of the service station, Ted held the gas hose and watched the meter.

"Any luck?" he asked.

"No."

"Any mail?"

"No. Acey Blodgett was in same time as Dan."

"Oh?"

"Seems it's Thursday, like Mrs. Purdy said."

Ted lifted his head as if he'd heard a shot. "Shit," he said. He clicked off the nozzle and squeezed it on again slowly, watching the meter hit fifty even before he hung up the hose. Then he looked at me. I was leaning against the front fender.

"You all right, kid? You want a drink?"

"No, thanks. I have to get back."

"Sure now?" He moved toward me but stopped a few feet away. I opened the cab door, and he went into the office and left money on the register. I put the magazine on the seat between us.

"He's probably waiting for you right now," Ted said as he started the truck. For a moment I thought he meant Dan.

"Oh, Magnus. Yes, he probably is."

The back of the population sign said, Leaving Mesa. Someone had shot a hole through the *M*. Ted glanced at me. I pressed my hands against the seat and closed my eyes, but the black afterimage of light panels floated across my vision. Better to watch the road.

Ted began to talk very low. "Easy, let it lie easy." He spoke softly as if to a green horse. "It takes time. Things mend." I've heard him talk like that to a frightened animal, running his hand across its body. "She's nothing, kid. Acey's nothing. Dan's been lonely."

I tried to focus on the mountains, but they were too far; it was easier to watch a thread caught under the wiper blade flick in the wind. "Let your hands work," he said. "The rest will fall away." My fist clamped around pain like a stone tool; I didn't want to hear him.

The road over the blue hood shimmered; my breath pushed around a constriction in my throat. Before the turnoff to the ranch, Ted looked over. "Ready?"

I nodded. We drove up the track without speaking, and he stopped by the steps with the motor running. I sat for a second, then picked up the magazine. I didn't see his face, but his hands were holding the wheel tight, as if he were pushing it away. I slid out.

"Thanks, Ted."

"Call if you need me."

"OK."

I walked past the house and headed up the path to my workshop. I hung my purse on the back of a wooden chair, and then, as if a bullet had hit me, I pressed my arms across my belly, curled my shoulders, and breathed in gasps. I don't know how long before the waves subsided, and I found myself watching a bar of sun angling through the slatted window onto the floor. This morning I had wanted to look at things from a new angle; now my head was raised, and there was no way to close the view.

The cloth I'd cut earlier lay on the table, a map of an alien landscape. Its folds were unfamiliar, ridges sheared off in sudden escarpments dropping to valleys with no rivers. I stared at the rumpled cloth, then slowly reached out and ran my finger along the cut edge. As if it were an unaccustomed act, I placed one piece on top of another, watching my fingers, willing them to move. I pushed a pin through the cloth.

I'd shut myself in this workroom long enough. Becky was right. It was time to turn around and look at that shadow running beside me. I leaned away from the table, my head back, and loosed a sound that filled the room as a canyon sometimes fills with a flood released in distant mountains by a storm long since passed. The sound fell away, and I heard silence close back.

I turned to the table, took up the green cloth, and began basting. Light had leached from the room when I finally laid the scissors down and left a needle woven into a half-finished seam. I went to the doorway and stretched my arms over my head. Low light in the valley was indiscriminate, without shadow or edge; for a moment, it weighed the same inside and out, flowing loose as air around me, a balance of dark and light, pain and absence of pain. A few stars began to show in the purple sky. Then the gleam of headlights slid across the flats, disappeared, and came back brighter as they turned toward the house. I walked down to wait by the bottom of the steps.

The headlights were gone, but their beams reached through space above me, sweeping the house and terrace. The truck's engine throbbed in the gully; gravel crackled under the wheels. Light blazed into my eyes and passed by. As Dan cut the motor, I went to the open window beside him.

"Dan, Magnus isn't here."

"No," he said. He looked ahead of him as if he were still driving. "No. Magnus is dead. I found him by the road the other side of Mesa. The buzzards had been to him already."

"Oh, Dan," I said.

He leaned his forehead against the steering wheel. I bent close without touching him. I could smell his sweat and the dust in his hair. I imagined spreading my hand over the dome of his head and pressing to ease him, to ease us both, through this hard beginning.

Coin

The sun comes into Tom's room all morning, and nowadays I leave the door open. It's a pleasant room, his maps and mineral samples still line his windowsill, each rock creating a separate shadow. Tom wrote he'd forgotten a few things, and would I send them along to him at college. His list is short this year, just two books and a small box from his bureau. The books are in the shelf over his desk: a history text and *The Concise Oxford Dictionary.* Philip gave the dictionary to Tom when he turned eighteen. On the flyleaf was the inscription: "To a man of few words, this might prove useful. Love, Dad."

The box on his bureau, Tom bought the year we spent Christmas in Martinique. He'd gone off with his father to the local market, and I'd stayed to sit in the sun and read. As they didn't often do things together, I was pleased. They brought back a straw basket full of tropical fruit, one of every kind in the market, Tom said. Philip had bought a wooden salad bowl and Tom, this box. It is made of tropical wood with a sunburst carved on the lid. The wood is close-grained, the workmanship crude.

When I pick up the box, it rattles. I get a couple of tissues to wrap the contents inside—two keys, a small bone-handled penknife, and an arrowhead. Underneath is a dime. It's bent in half, folded diagonally across the torch. The serrated edges don't quite meet. I pick it up and remember how it came to be bent, what happened before.

Five years ago. A Thursday. I know because that's trash pickup day. The truck trundles along the street with the men hanging on behind. When it stops, they fan out and drag garbage cans and plastic bundles from the ends of the driveways to dump in the hopper at the back. The men shout, banging the side of the truck with shovels to signal the driver to move on. That Thursday they hadn't come by yet. The kitchen was still quiet; Philip was in the dining room. Every morning, he shaves and showers and comes to breakfast wearing his red plaid robe over his underwear. On cold mornings like that one was, he wears black knee socks. He sat at the table reading the paper folded back in a column, very neat, as if he were on a commuter train. I prefer to spread the pages out on the table so I can drink my coffee, eat my toast, and read at the same time.

I was in the kitchen making an omelette, working fast. Although it was time for Tom to leave, there was no particular hurry for me; I'd stopped fixing his breakfast several months ago when he said he preferred to make his own. He hadn't come down yet, and I was determined not to call him again. The egg shells were brittle that morning, and bits got into the bowl. The trash was overflowing, and when I dropped the shells on top, they rolled onto the floor. Tom was supposed to carry the trash out every day, but it must have been four days since he'd last emptied the basket. I didn't grumble aloud, glad that Philip was reading. It didn't take much to set him off in those days, especially where Tom was concerned. I was anxious for Tom to get off to school without a fuss.

Then I heard Tom on the stairs and coming through the dining room. He looked terrible. Actually, he looked normal, but he didn't match my image of a high school freshman. His hair was rumpled, and even though I'd left a clean pair on his bed, he had on the same jeans he'd worn all week. His black T-shirt was too big for him. It had a picture of a guitar player and the band's name in ugly yellow lettering.

Philip must have heard Tom's footsteps. They have a distinctive sound, even in running shoes; nothing he did then was exactly quiet. Philip never moved the paper, just glanced over it and said, "Garbage."

Tom kept walking into the kitchen and opened the refrigerator door.

"Hi," I said. "You'd better hurry."

"I'll just make lunch. Are there any Cokes, Mom?"

"On the second shelf behind the lettuce, and there's apples in the drawer."

Then Philip said it again. "Garbage."

Tom had hold of the peanut butter jar. For a moment, he hesitated in his swing around to the counter, before he hunched his shoulder against the door and clicked it closed. He turned and took two slices of bread and began to spread on peanut butter—thick. Philip got up and stood in the doorway holding the paper with his finger between the pages he had been reading. It was still folded in the long, neat column.

"I've spoken to you twice," he said.

Tom did not turn around. "You talking to me?"

"You know damned well I am."

"Oh, you didn't say so."

"You know damned well what I mean, and look at me when you speak to me."

"I don't even know the color of your eyes."

That was crazy of Tom to say. Philip's eyes are light blue, but right now they were the color of needles. His nostrils widened and he breathed hard.

"Get the garbage!"

"What do you mean?"

"Get it!"

"You get it."

"Dammit, I'll thrash you."

When Philip gets mad, he gets formal. I sometimes expect him to say "Zounds!" Tom began to laugh. His shoulders were shaking, and a glob of peanut butter fell off the knife. I wasn't watching Philip, but the next moment I could see his black leather slipper moving in an upward arc. I noticed how shapely his calf was, how his toe was pointed. It caught Tom in the seam of his jeans and kind of lifted him up for a second. He turned. Philip was crouched slightly, weight forward, arms bent and away from his body.

"Fuck you!" Tom said.

Philip dropped the paper and snapped his hand behind his shoulder; then, as if throwing something heavy, he leaned into a punch. Tom ducked under the fist and ran. He jerked open the front door and was down the steps into the street. Philip went after him, his red robe flying open. He looked like a big bird crossing the lawn. The garbage truck was just pulling up in front of the house, the men hanging on behind. One yelled at Tom, "Run, boy, run. Your Daddy's going to get you."

The driver with grizzled grey hair leaned out the window and yelled at Philip, "You get him, Daddy. You show him."

The men waved their arms and laughed. Tom and Philip beat past them and down the street. Philip was fast and was closing in on Tom when a car stopped at the corner. It was Jeremy, a senior in Tom's school who sometimes gave him a lift. He must have taken in what was happening because he opened the door on the passenger side. Tom jumped in, and they spun off before Philip reached the corner. He stood and watched the car pull away, fists on his hips. I could see his shoulders heave with each breath. He pulled his robe around him and tightened his belt, then walked back up the street looking at his feet. The trash truck had moved on before he reached the house. I held the front door open as he came inside. In the kitchen, he picked the paper up off the floor.

"You almost caught up with him," I said.

"Almost," he said. Then with the paper bunched in his hand, he went upstairs, clunking his feet on each step.

The omelette batter had settled in the bowl. I covered it with plastic, wrapped the sandwiches Tom had started to make, and put them away in the refrigerator. I poured myself a cup of coffee and sat at the table thinking about Tom's eyes when he turned on his father. There was surprise there, and anger, but also a tiny lift under his eyes, like relief. A kind of envy swelled up in me—that delicate, almost pretty movement of Philip's leg, the powerful intimacy of the act.

It was strange, but that was the beginning of something different between them. The following weekend, Philip asked Tom to help him get firewood. There had been a storm, and the road crew had cut up a fallen tree a few blocks away. The two of them went out in the car and filled the trunk with logs. I was planting bulbs in random clusters at the edge of the lawn when they came back.

They didn't talk much. Tom unloaded the wood, and Philip split the big logs with a wedge and sledge hammer. He'd lift the hammer high, then rise up at the top of the swing and bring it down fast and easy. The only sign of effort was a little push at the end of each stroke. The wedge would dig in, and the log would crack and strain until it fell into two pieces exposing pink grain and loosening the acrid smell of oak. Tom took the halved logs to split into fireplace size with an ax.

Philip stood for a moment watching Tom. "Don't choke the handle. Hold the end. Let its weight work for you," he said.

Tom's ax skidded on the edge of the log slicing off a strip of bark.

"My aim's lousy," Tom said.

"Line the log with a crack running toward you. Keep your eye on that. You'll get it."

Philip leaned back and put his hand in his pocket. He pulled out a coin and set it on the center of the upended log.

"Try for that."

Tom made several attempts, but the coin bounced off when he hit to one side or the other. "Hell, you do it."

Philip set up the log and centered the coin. He paused holding the ax in front of him, then he reached up, rose on the balls of his feet, and brought the ax down. The log cracked in two pieces joined at the bottom by a couple of inches of splintered wood. Philip let the haft go and stood back. Tom leaned over to lift out the ax. The coin was bent in half around the blade.

"Jesus!" Tom said.

"It's not good for the blade," Philip said.

They worked the rest of the morning, fetching several more loads which they cut and stacked between two pines.

I turn the coin over in my palm then put it back in the wooden box. I'll mail it later with the books. Tom's lucky; now that he's left home, he can pack parts of his life away. When you live with someone a long time and keep on living with them, things don't compact easily. Beginnings and endings stretch like cable strands that twist around one another; you hardly notice if a single filament has changed.

I look out the window at our present woodpile. It's in the same place between the pines, but the logs are smaller. We get them from a man who brings them in a pickup. He and Philip unload it, throwing the logs into a pile, then they have a beer and lean against the truck and talk for a while. Later Philip splits and stacks the wood. The pile should last all winter.

Lately we've taken to having Sunday breakfast in front of a fire. Philip spreads the paper on a low table, and we have coffee in mugs and make fireplace toast. We don't say much, but read out bits of the paper to each other. When I finish the book section, I hand it to him in exchange for the editorials. Sometimes when I'm reading, he glances over at me. I don't need to look up. Philip's eyes are pale blue; mine, like Tom's, are deep brown. I pour him another cup of coffee.

Domain

Crow calls, loud and insistent, break through the quiet. I turn from my easel to see a flock swirl over the meadow in a loose spiral. Last night, a high wind took most of the leaves from the woods exposing the bones of the land, and now low sun picks out the contours. I stand back and look at the canvas. The composition begins to take shape. I've laid down underpainting in wide strokes of ocher and blue, feeling out space and the ridge's mass. I am not ready to stop work, but Walt is coming, and I don't want to be painting when he arrives. I rinse my brushes in turpentine, dry them on a rag, and set them in a stoneware jug.

Walt must have been at the office when he called this morning, it was after nine. He said he had a business meeting in Harrisburg and was driving past on the interstate, could he stop in around five? Fine, I said, come for dinner. I haven't seen him since he and Midge were here one Sunday shortly after I moved. They were checking the place out.

Although the cabin isn't her style, Midge said, "It's great for you, Ellie." And she's right. Walt tapped the paneling, inspected the fuse box, the well. He wanted to see the land—my domain, he called it. We'd gone for a walk, but Midge had on the wrong shoes, so we came back a short way by road.

Things take time in the country, and it was almost a year before the phone was installed, but Midge and I exchanged postcards every few weeks. I had no word from Walt; he's not one to write. I didn't mind the absence of a phone; silence is a kind of privacy, and that was what I needed. Midge was the first person I called when the phone was finally connected. We've been chatting for twenty-five years; it was as if there had been no gap. Amy was bringing the baby for a visit; she'd fixed the sewing room as a nursery. She asked how Allen was getting along in college.

"And your work?" This was a real question. Midge has an eye I trust. At my second show, she bought a small oil of Patrick's hiking boots that is as good as anything I did before I stopped painting three years ago. It was odd talking to her again; I felt vaguely disoriented as if calling home while traveling.

I hang my painting shirt on a nail and close the door to my workroom. I've always needed a private place to paint. When we bought our house after we were married, Patrick had a studio fixed for me in the attic with a northern skylight and sloping walls. When he'd get home from the office, he'd thump up the stairs and stand by the door watching me paint. I would work on, but my focus was gone. "How's it going?" he'd ask. If I tried to talk about the work, it sounded stiff. Patrick would pretend to listen, but after a bit he'd say, "Come down for a beer." That's when I would have to decide. If I said no, he'd shrug and go off; I'd have a hard time getting back to work. Usually I went with him.

After the reviews of my first show, Patrick hung three of my paintings in his office. He had them expensively framed and lit with hidden spots, although I don't think he liked them much. He certainly didn't like my artist friends. I found it easier to see them during the day and be downstairs when he came home. Gradually he stopped coming up to the studio.

One Saturday three years ago, I heard him on the stairs; he came and stood by the door. He didn't say anything for a long time, but in spite of his presence, I was able to concentrate and kept working. Then, instead of asking me down for a beer, he said he wanted a divorce. He said there was a woman he wanted to marry. My brush moved across the canvas, I didn't think or speak, I didn't notice him leave. The light began to fade, but I kept painting until all I could see were tones of grey. When it was dark, I sat listening to the beat inside my head.

The weeks that followed I remember like an illness, as if I were outside myself. I see a woman, arms crossed, rocking slightly, staring through windows grey with rain. I let the pain ripen, and only much later did I compare notes with recently divorced friends. We dissected details of our betrayals: dinner charged at a restaurant we'd not been to, a new tie, movie ticket stubs. It was so trite.

Walt and Midge were there for me after Patrick moved out. Midge called every day, and Walt would stop on his way home for a drink. He helped me find a lawyer, advised me on money matters, and suggested I try the art institute for a teaching job. I knew he saw Patrick. They had been college roommates, and Patrick is Walt's best friend, but it's always been an unbalanced exchange. Walt was the one who would suggest a weekend at their beach house or come up with tickets to a ball game. Patrick didn't seem to notice, or perhaps he didn't want the responsibility of a best friend. I was glad of Walt's connection with Patrick. I wanted to hear his name spoken, and I cherished my spurts of anger as if they kept something alive.

In those first weeks, I looked forward to Walt's visits. I'd get out ice and have cheese or dip ready. Walt is a big man and filled a good bit of space when he entered a room. We talked easily about things we never had before; maybe he was different without Patrick there. One night I asked him how he felt about what Patrick had done.

"Like hell," he said. "As if I had done it myself; I know how the guy feels." He got up and poured another drink.

The next night, he kissed me before he left, a real kiss. I was diverted by my body's response and didn't listen to what he said as he went out. The next evening he didn't come. The wedge of brie flattened and spread in a thick smooth spill. At seven, I turned on the news, then watched a game show, a rerun of *M*A*S*H*, and on through to a late movie from the '40s about a British war widow. Only when I was in bed did I recall what he said as he left. "A near miss, Ellie." The next day, he sent flowers, a formal arrangement in a thick glass bowl wrapped in plastic. The card read, "As always, W."

Soon after, I started teaching at the institute—drawing and a composition course. Allen was still home, and he and his high school friends kept the place noisy; I kept them fed. The next fall, he went off to college. I felt strange not being able to paint, as if I were a cheat. But my classes went well. I liked teaching and I liked my colleagues. They had jug wine parties where an autumnal haze of marijuana blued the studio. I'd join a friend for a drink at a bar, but I always came home alone. One morning in the mirror, I saw a woman playing the divorced artist. I winced with embarrassment and the next weekend drove out to the country. I began to look at farms and houses for sale and imagined living in them.

Following an ad in the paper, I found this place—a cabin, set against the edge of woods, facing over fields and farmlands with the Appalachians stretching in blue ridges beyond. I wanted it. With a kind of blind assurance, I sold the house and bought the cabin. In one liberating month, I discarded furniture, dishes, clothes, letters, anything that threatened to weigh me down with more than I needed. There is no attic here.

I put off clearing out the studio until the house was almost empty. Since Patrick left, I hadn't used it. The canvas I painted that last night was turned against the wall. I set it on the easel. A heavy black disc almost covered the surface. It was built with pigment laid layer on layer, and from under it leaked a narrow halo of orange, sienna, white, alizarin. In the early dusk, the canvas generated its own glow, a clear burn. I began to pack brushes, charcoal, unstretched canvasses. I knew I would paint again.

The cabin is gold now in the low sun; the glass doors to the deck are open. On the table, the chrysanthemums have dropped tawny petals around the base of a pewter mug. I throw out the wilted flowers and rinse away their acrid smell. From the window over the sink, I see a car turn off the valley road. I dry my hands, check the casserole in the oven, shake out the blue tablecloth, and set a bowl of oranges on it. Behind the house, a car crunches on the gravel, a door slams. I go onto the deck.

"Ellie!" Walt is smoother than I remember, more kempt—tweed jacket, blue shirt, tie—a magazine ad. Was my old life like that?

"Hello, Walt. Welcome." My voice is flat, far away. I want him to stand still so I can hold him in focus, but he starts up the steps. His face gets bigger; there's grey in his wiry eyebrows, the faint smell of aftershave. He kisses my cheek. I step back, unused to anyone so close.

"You look great," he says, "different." Walt's eyes are

ultramarine. "So this is it?" He is still looking at me.

I swing around to the meadow. "My domain."

I don't want Walt in the cabin yet. "Let's walk now while we still have the sun," I say.

He holds out a bottle of wine, a vintage claret.

"Lovely," I say. "I hope the meal is worthy. Let me put it inside and get the clippers. I want to cut some leaves."

When I come out, he is leaning on the rail. "There aren't many leaves left."

"I'll find seed pods; they last all winter."

We follow the ruts of a farm track. "My land runs to the fence," I say, "but I walk on my neighbor's fields, trade hay for good will."

"You ought to get something for it," he says. "Hay's worth money."

"It's no good yet. I'm trying to bring the fields back. They were let go for years. Next summer's crop may be better."

"Don't be had, Ellie."

"I won't."

I stop to clip empty milkweed pods and dried Queen Anne's lace. An animal trail slopes through close-growing sumac to the edge of the woods. The path is narrow; I lead. Once inside the woods, we can see far through the bare trees. Smooth beech trunks rise out of fallen yellow leaves; space is filled with light as if it comes from the ground.

"You fit this place," Walt says from behind me.

At the bottom of the draw, the path crosses a small stream. Ferns arc over the bank, the moss edging it still green. I glance up and stop. Sprawled across the trickle of water lies the body of a young deer, its legs splayed, its muzzle in the water. The open eyes are milky as opals.

Walt stops beside me. A leaf breaks off with a click and drifts down; it seems a long way to the meadow.

"It's been shot," I say.

A dark thread of blood twists from a hole in its shoulder. Black hoofs, clean and dainty, shine among the pebbles.

"It came for water," I say. There is a cold earthy smell as if a door were open in the ground.

"Ellie," Walt says, "let's go."

"Wait." I reach out to touch the grey winter coat of its flank.

"Don't," he says. "Leave it. We can't do anything."

I feel him tug my hand. The dried flowers have fallen in the water below, and the deer seems to reach for the bouquet only everything is slightly wrong.

"Come away." Walt, on the other bank now, pulls me behind him. I follow him up through the woods toward the meadow. Two squirrels spiral down a hickory trunk, their feet scrabbling against loose bark. We break out from the trees onto a field of winter wheat; its vivid green seems too strong for the muted landscape. We edge the woods in single file. I push my hands into my sweater pockets.

"It'll be gone by spring," I say. "Only bones and scattered hair."

"Don't worry, Ellie, it's nothing." He walks with his head down watching the ground. Where the wheat field ends, we rejoin the farm track.

"I'll show you the cliffs; they're this way, across the fence and through the pasture," I say.

"Good, there'll be room here to walk beside you." Walt swings his legs over the gate and lands with spring enough to take his weight easily. I'd forgotten how well he moves. Patrick, the fisherman and skier, had a tentative quality to his actions, as if he had to think first. We walk slowly. Walt gives me news of old friends; I hear myself tell about my life.

"There's an A & P, a farm co-op, the post office. Paints and books I order by mail. Nice neighbors, country people. My work? Different; better than where I left off."

The hill steepens; it takes our breath, and we climb in silence. At the top, grass gives way to an outcrop of bedrock that shears off, and the view opens. I come often to this place. Today the sky is a harsh Prussian blue over the hills. A hawk, barely visible against the ridge, balances on a rising thermal; its presence gives substance to the space. I recall how yellow light in the woods congealed around the fallen deer.

"Is this why you moved here?" Walt is looking across the valley.

"Partly," I say. "I wanted this place before I knew I wanted it." The hawk has risen and holds against the sky.

"I guess we all have things like that," Walt says. "Things we don't realize we want."

The hawk leans, angling down fast. I lose it a moment, then catch it again over a white silo. Walt is watching me, not asking anything, but I know I will have to decide.

We're quiet on the way home. I think of the black hooves

suspended over water. We left too fast, before air could move again, before color returned to the moss.

A circle of cold enters the cabin with us.

"I'll start a fire," Walt says.

"Kindling and paper are in the wood box."

Walt used to rearrange the logs in our fireplace; Patrick would watch him, but say nothing. The paper flares, and a puff of smoke backs into the room. Walt slides the front door open to let it disperse.

"Can I get you a drink?" he asks.

"Sure. Bourbon's on the counter. You'll need ice."

The kitchen is small. Walt sets the glasses next to where I am slicing cheese. The hair on the back of his wrist is dark. I have stopped cutting to watch the narrow isthmus between us. As he pours the whiskey, his hand almost brushes mine.

I reach for a plate. "Just a splash of water."

"I remember," Walt says.

We take our drinks to armchairs by the fire. I set the cheese on a low table between us. Then I ask about Patrick.

"We have lunch downtown, the two of us mostly." He and Midge know Elaine, of course.

"Did he ask you to check on me?" I say this without thinking and realize the answer no longer matters.

"No, I came for myself."

A draft slides through the half-opened door, and I reach back to close it. The hills are slate blue against the sky.

"I like this time of year," I say. "Edges are sharp. You want doors open or shut."

"Sometimes it's good to let edges blur, let things happen," Walt says.

"No." I stand up with my back toward him holding my hands, palms out, to the fire. A log snaps; I hear him set down his glass. "Does Midge know you're here?" I ask.

"Whoa! What's this about? What have I said?"

"Nothing. You never do. You just set it up, then wait for things to happen, so it's not your fault when they do."

I hear him get up and walk away.

"OK, I'll tell you something," he says. "I've thought about this for years. I thought maybe it would happen at the beach house, or we'd go off somewhere that neither of us knows. A country motel."

"With no before and no after."

"Right. What's wrong with that?"

"Nothing's wrong with it. I was glad when you called. I thought we'd laugh and drink wine; I thought we might go to bed. But it doesn't just happen. I decide; you decide. It's a choice. When you tell me you haven't said a thing, it ends up charged to my credit card."

All the time, I am holding my hands up to the fire.

"OK, El," Walt's voice is right behind me. "I've decided."

I turn carefully, knowing how close he is. "So have I." We face each other without touching. I let myself see Walt as if he has just arrived. I let welcome unfold around us, then step back.

"Hey, how about opening that wine?"

After dinner, Walt and I do the dishes. We take our time. He hands me a plate hot and wet from the rinse water. I wipe it dry and stack it on the shelf, then turn back for another. Everything draws out like that, dinner, our talk; even the wine lasts a long time.

Later I reach over, and, as if in abeyance from my body, my fingers slide across the ridges of his hand into a cleft between his knuckles. He raises my hand; the small tug of his kiss releases a familiar spill of pleasure. We make love slowly with the assurance of old friends.

I wake trying to catch the threads of a dispersing dream. Beside me, Walt inhales silently, then breathes out with a light urgent sigh. The warmth of his body, the ease of my own, the fragmented dream merge. I smile. It's been a long time since I shared a bed.

A need to reclaim the cabin stirs. I disengage from the covers, and stepping over Walt's clothes, I unhook my wrapper and close the door behind me. The living room is grey, toneless as an unlit stage set; the windows appear to open on white walls. I have not seen the cabin in this light before. I pull my robe around me and cross my arms against the chill. The gesture loosens a memory of the attic studio: light gone, Patrick gone, a cave hollowed in my belly. I hold my breath making space for pain, but the wave withdraws, and I am left quite still.

Outside the glass doors, fog twists through the deck railing, blanking meadow and wood. I can see only the silhouette of a leafless apple tree, no ridge to align direction, no shadow to mark the time. This is the place I chose to be.

I switch on a lamp. Color returns to the room: garnet rug, blue table cloth, bowl of oranges. The ashes are still warm as I stir the coals to rebuild the fire. At the kitchen counter, I measure coffee and water into a white enamel pot. The place is tidy; I recall washing up with Walt. I set the coffee to heat and return to the fireplace stretching my arms over my head. My sleeves fall back, and inside my wrapper my body is taut, content. The door behind me opens. Walt is fully dressed and, except that he needs a shave, trim as ever.

"Good morning, El." He kisses my shoulder from behind and puts his arm around my belly. We stand rocking lightly in front of the fire.

"I was going to light it for you," he says.

"It's OK. I do it every day."

Walt moves to the fireplace and resettles a log with the tongs. "I have a meeting in two hours." He turns and looks around the cabin. "God, I want to stay," he says.

"Well, have some coffee."

I fill two mugs from the pot and set his on the counter. He pours milk and walks to the window.

"It's a thick one." Walt, outlined against the fog, rubs a hand down the back of his head. "No regrets?"

"Regrets? I feel terrific." I lean back to the fire's warmth. "Terrific."

"You're going to be all right, El."

"I already am."

We drink our coffee; the fire crackles.

"I have to go." But he stays looking out at the white fog. "I'll call later and stop on my way back."

"No," I say. "Don't call."

"Why not? It was wonderful."

"Walt, I'm glad you came. I'm glad you stayed, but it won't hold. Light shifts, things change."

I cannot see his face against the window. He sets his mug on the sill and comes to where I am.

"I want more." He is not smiling. His head is lifted, and he looks at me as I would at my own face for a self-portrait, then he nods. "You're right, El."

I touch his cheek; he takes my hand and holds it against his mouth then slides the door open and crosses the deck. By the bottom step, he is already a generalized outline in the fog. The car turns, its red taillights visible a perceptible second after its shape disappears.

I know what I am going to do. I will take a sketch book and go down through the beech woods and record the deer's blank eyes, its loss of grace, its absence of fear. Later, when the fog burns off, I will start laying color on a big canvas.

Roxy

The spider plant had filled out since we took over its care two months earlier; arced shoots sprouted tufts of striped leaves, then white worm roots. I was misting the plants in the window, and Christy, stretched on the sofa, was reading the *Cheyenne Free Press*. My father sent me a subscription when I came East to college. "So you won't forget where you're from," he wrote. But it's Christy who reads the cattle prices, rainfall charts, and rodeo announcements.

I don't think about home much. Occasionally a whiff of pine bark mulch from the plantings outside the museum jolts me back to the mountains, and once in the ladies room of a classy restaurant, the marble stalls were the exact orange tones of the canyon below the ranch. I lost a few minutes thinking about sage flats and the sound of my mare's hoofs. It shifted the whole evening for me.

"Roxy!" Christy sat up. "Listen to this: 'Isobel Hooper, fifty-two-year-old housewife atop La Torre after a solo ascent of the treacherous north face.' I didn't know your mother was a mountain climber."

I swiveled around. "I didn't either. Let's see."

Christy handed me the folded paper. There she was, my mother: rolled sweatband low on her forehead, a coil of rope over her shoulder, and her eyes as wild as the mountains behind her. A cast in her left eye gives her a manic look that people interpret as enthusiasm, but it's there whether she's checking pantyhose for a run or assessing the quality of an opal. My mother deals in semiprecious stones, handles them is more accurate. She does it for pleasure, not business, although it keeps her in travel funds. She's been around the world on her search trips, and two years ago she brought me with her.

My father claims she took up mineralogy because someone in freshman geology said she looked sinister wearing a loupe. Her activities are triggered by chance remarks like that. Last winter, she read Shakespeare for reference to gems after a discussion with some guy about the pearl, or whatever, in the Ethiop's ear. She wrote an article and sent it to the Elizabethan Society. They published it in their journal; I only got a B minus in English lit. that semester.

The story was written by a reporter who went on a weekend climb in the park: "Our party, led by a professional guide, ascended the peak of La Torre via the south col., a 5.5 pitch recommended for advanced intermediate climbers. We were resting on the summit when Ms. Hooper appeared over the north rim. She lay face down on the rock, then sat up and said, 'I didn't expect witnesses.' This was her first major solo, and although an experienced hiker, she had been rock climbing for less than a year." The article went on to discuss the number and expense of rescue operations occasioned by inexperienced climbers.

"It's Tony's fault."

My younger brother, Tony, went to mountaineering school a couple of summers ago. I thought it was just another macho summer camp, but it indoctrinated him. He came back with this reverence for mountains.

"What's wrong with climbing?" Christy said. "My mother won't break out of the house long enough to throw a snowball."

I like Christy's mother. She sewed name tapes on all Christy's college clothes, and she tutors inner-city kids.

"There's nothing wrong with it," I said. "It's that she does it so easily. I bet all she told Dad was, 'I climbed La Torre today.' He'd flip a page of *The Cattle Breeder* and say, 'I hope the weather was fine.'"

"So? She does what she wants; he doesn't interfere."

"Well, he should."

"What do you mean?" Christy looked at me as if I'd said something outrageous, but she's right, I don't know what I mean.

I used to wish Dad would tell her to quit her expeditions and stay home, but instead he learned to cook and showed me how to make ragout and key lime pie. "Your mother has her own way of doing what she needs to do," he said.

Even at home, my mother goes after things. She'll open

the *Britannica* flat during dinner to ascertain a point. If she's right, she'll nod silently and close the book; if she's wrong, she says, "I was mistaken," then reads the article to correct her lapse. I'll say this for her, she always listens, although there are times I wished she'd just say, "Yes, dear," like other mothers.

Christy was reading again.

"Remember when Brad met her?" I said. "He talked about her for days and kept looking at me crooked as if I was supposed to be different because she was my mother."

She had come to visit me in the co-op house where I live at college. During dinner, she got talking with Brad about the significance of treasure or something. Brad was on dish crew that night, and she followed him into the kitchen so they could keep talking. Later he said what a powerful roving mind she had, what connections. Connections! She makes them up as she goes along and then never thinks about them again.

I was moving around the room touching things: the white summer slipcovers, a jade ashtray, the porcelain cockatoo in the window. We are staying in Christy's grandmother's apartment for the summer in exchange for keeping the plants watered and the place dusted. We're pretty good about it and have kept to the letter of the rule, no gentleman callers overnight. Christy and Brad claim if they get in after twelve, it's not overnight.

I turned over the Chinese bronze puppy I was holding. It was the size of my palm. Etched in the flat bottom of its feet were little pads with tiny circles for claws. I ran my finger over them and set it back on the table. No one would know the lines were there.

I wanted something and walked through the dining room into the dim kitchen. The refrigerator door opened like a grotto; light shone through jars of orange and cranberry juice and glinted off a green soda can. Once when I was little, I woke in the night and came downstairs and saw my mother in front of the open refrigerator. She stood there for a long time, then closed the door without taking anything out or putting anything in. When she turned, she saw me and said. "Well, hello." I asked what she was doing. "I thought I might find something I wanted, but I don't seem hungry after all." She picked me up and hugged me. "Your feet are cold." She nuzzled my neck. "Maybe I'll eat you," she said.

There was nothing I wanted either, so I shut the door and went back to the living room. Christy was on the phone telling Brad about my mother.

"You could do a piece," she was saying. Brad is taking a writing workshop at The New School and everything has a story in it for him.

I went to my room. I wanted to talk with Tony, but he was working on a dude ranch in the Tetons, besides he'd be pleased. He doesn't feel the same way I do about our mother. They have a connection that I don't. Sometimes I'd feel like an extra with them, although neither Tony nor my mother seemed to notice. But Tony's getting wise. He's away from home this summer and is coming East to college.

I went to the window and opened it wide. It looks over the park and is high enough to take in a lot of sky. The air was heavy, the overcast a generalized grey, with no break to show separate clouds. After a while, I went down the hall and called to Christy that I was going out.

"Hey, wait a minute." She came from her room wrapped in one of her grandmother's huge white towels. "Brad's coming over; he wants to talk about Isobel. He wants to do an interview with her, like a profile. A ranging piece. *The Voice* might take it."

"He can call for an appointment. Dry Springs, Wyoming."

"I told him she lived there. He said the call would be an investment."

"Safer than high yield bonds."

"Hey, are you all right?" Christy was squinting at me as if I were a long way off with the light behind me.

"I'm going out. A movie maybe."

"Hold on. I'll come with you."

She would, too. She'd leave a note for Brad saying we were at the movies. I shifted gears. "It's OK. I'm fine."

"You sure?"

"Yes."

Outside I paused on the corner. I didn't want to deal with trees or sky, so I turned away from the park. In spite of having no particular destination, I was walking fast.

Tony said mountain climbing was concentration. You don't think about reaching the top. You know how every muscle moves; your hand reads the texture of rock, and once you start, you can't pull out. Like the gate clicking behind you in a roller coaster. I can see for Tony it's kind of practicing, but why my mother?

A black stretch limo blocked the crossing and as I passed in front of it I tapped its fender without looking at the driver. I thought of my mother's hand on warm rock inching toward a crevice. What did she need to prove?

On the corner of Broadway, I stopped at a cafe where I sometimes go and ordered coffee and a Danish. The blue Formica table was still wet from being wiped off. I lined the napkin dispenser with the salt and pepper. I wanted to do something—walk across the Verrazano Bridge, canoe around Manhattan, something I could finish. To break a commitment leaves you different, even a dumb promise to yourself. Was being a daughter a kind of commitment? I hadn't chosen it.

The waiter put down the coffee and Danish. I tore a sugar packet across a picture of a covered bridge. The crystals seemed coarser than usual, as if they were close to my eyes. Someone had left a paper on the seat folded back to the entertainment section. A box showed the profile of a city with a moon over it: Enthralling, Captivating. The movie was playing at the Quad a few blocks away with three other films at the same house. That's what I'd do, take in a movie, take in all four on only one ticket. A Guinness record. I knew the rules: see the movies all the way around but not necessarily from the beginning; record title, actors, time, place, a sentence about the story.

I circled the show times. The essence of the operation was to avoid notice, look ordinary; don't buy food, the popcorn seller could remember my face.

"Can I order a turkey on whole wheat?"

I must have jerked it out fast. The man behind the counter stopped drying a glass and looked at me for a second before he said, "Sure."

"To go, please."

"To go."

I stashed the packet in my canvas bag and started downtown. It was dumb, but I had a sense of purpose as I walked, like the time I set out with my mother and Tony to look for an abandoned garnet mine. We knew what we were after; I carried the lunches in my backpack and felt responsible for the whole world. We never got to the mine. I was disappointed, but neither Tony nor my mother cared. He found an elk skull with the antler still attached, and they carried it between them down the trail.

Heat radiated from the sidewalk; the air was thick. At the crossing, bottle caps, flip tops, a paper clip, and a button were embedded in the tar like fossils.

I bought a ticket, and an usher at the door tore it in half. The theater downstairs was almost full, only a few seats in the front, but I like that. Tony and I used to sit in the second row whenever our mother left us off for the Saturday matinee. I realized I hadn't been to a movie by myself before. I set my elbows exactly halfway on the armrest and pulled out the small memo book my father had given me to keep notations of my expenses, but only the first three pages had been used. I wrote down the movie title, the place, and the time.

The house darkened, a no-smoking sign wobbled across the curtain. The feature eased in with a shot of a doorway that drew back to row houses on a shabby street, then up over the city until we saw hills and rivers and bays like the view from a mountain. The film cut to downtown offices letting out, a surge of people going home. A man walking fast passes a woman who watches his grip shift on the handle of his briefcase. The movie ends with a shot of the doorway again, ajar. A cat slides out and sits on the top step staring toward the street. The cast list unrolls across the placid cat too fast to read completely.

After the audience cleared, I moved to the end of the row and checked the paper. Twenty minutes until the movie across the lobby began. Piano music for the intermission was Schubert, short and unobtrusive. I tried to write "This film is about . . .," but I'm not good at the broad view. Instead I wrote of a scene where a bee whines around while they cook hamburgers in the backyard. The woman keeps watching it so she doesn't have to hear what the man says. The story was too neat; things don't end simply.

The preview came on again, and as I left, I passed a few latecomers but no usher. In the ladies room, I waited in a booth. I had a scene in my mind, but it wasn't from the movie. It was in Kashmir the summer I traveled with my mother. We were in the jewelry bazaar, a warren of little open-front shops. My mother had pulled out her little notebook computer to figure some question of exchange. In a nearby booth, an old man with a white turban sat cross-legged on a rug sorting stones in a tray. He watched my mother punch the keys, then he beckoned her over holding his palm upward to show that she should look at his stones. He pushed a few into a pile and pointed at the computer indicating he wanted to trade. My mother touched the stones, stirring them with the tip of her finger. I don't think they were particularly good stones. He brushed a few more into the pile; my mother shook her head. I knew she liked the computer; Tony had given it to her. The old man added more, but she refused again. Finally he shrugged, hollowing his chest and arms as if he had nothing to meet the computer's worth.

My mother lifted her chin and looked at his face. The pause was long enough for me to wonder if he'd said something I did not hear, then she set the computer on the tray in front of him. "Here," she said, "you may have it." As if he understood her words, he bowed, then swung around to a small safe behind him and took out a handful of little silk pouches with tasseled drawstrings. He put them on the tray next to the computer. Without smiling, she bowed back. "Thank you," she said and picked up the sacks.

Later at the hotel, she loosened the strings and opened the bags spilling out agates, amethysts, garnets, moonstones, and tiger eyes. They were top quality stones; when my mother sold them back in the States, she got enough to buy herself a used telescope. I asked her once if she felt badly about the trade. "No," she said, "it wasn't a trade. We both knew it was a gift."

Things like that happen to my mother, and she's not surprised. I would have felt like a cheat whenever I thought about it.

People began to enter the rest room. I left the booth and joined a line in the lobby. The usher was talking to a woman and barely glanced at us. I took a seat halfway down with space around me. I unpacked the turkey sandwich and regretted not having brought a Coke. When I tried to remember the last film, it seemed as if I'd seen it weeks ago.

The same preview came on. I felt I was watching from outside myself, seeing secondhand. The movie began with the spare lines of an English landscape behind the titles, the colors pale, almost sepia, like an Atget photograph with the same disturbing undertones. The camera holds on an isolated farmstead. As an old woman entered the courtyard, I became aware of something touching me. I turned my eyes. A hand curved around my breast, a man's hand, long fingered with broad knuckles and wiry hair. It rested lightly. Without moving my head, I glanced sideways; he was watching the screen, his right arm stretched across his chest. He looked ordinary, nice. He may have sensed my glance or maybe my eyes reflected light when they moved because he turned and looked directly at me. I may have smiled, I don't know.

"Get your hand off me," I said it loud so people heard. A woman behind me leaned forward.

"Move, you bastard. Leave her alone."

I started to get up, but the woman put her hand on my shoulder. "Make him move, the creep."

He was already at the end of the row and starting up the aisle. I turned and smiled at the woman, and in the same instant I was angry for feeling grateful. I watched the rest of the movie impatient with its diffused images, the artful tightening of focus on a flower or a woman's gesture.

During the intermission, I stayed in my seat, but looked around for the man who had touched me. He had gone. It was almost as if he had been part of the film. I tried to remember the feel of his hand, but recalled only the mounded knuckles, the stiff hair. Then, as if my foot had slipped on a rock, I felt a jolt of fear. I must stay alert, recognize danger. I touched the rough canvas of my bag and glanced at my watch.

The lobby was empty as I pushed through the padded door of the neighboring theater. It was a Brazilian film in brash color, the print flawed, the subtitles unsteady. From the first shot of neon lights and carnival faces, I loved it. Dead backcountry plazas combust when a troupe of traveling entertainers enter. These strange, fierce people carry life with them. In one scene, camped on the edge of a jungle river, they look up and find a half circle of Indians watching them from the bank above. The Indians are silent, their spears rest on the ground. Slowly the conjurer stands, his hand stretched to the side; he spreads the first two fingers. A white ball appears in the V. We see him do it again and again until all his fingers hold balls between them. As we watch, we are connected—Indians, traveling players, and audience.

I was suddenly hungry. I rifled my bag for the last of the sandwich. When the movie was over, I waited as the theater emptied. My mother was like the conjurer, she could make you believe what was happening was the center of the whole world; I'm one of the people on the plaza who watch and afterward turn back to their houses somehow a little changed.

It was enough. I went outside and hailed a cab for the short ride home.

In the kitchen, I drank orange juice from the jar. Christy had propped a note on the counter next to Brad's knapsack: "Good night, Roxy."

It was late when I woke. Flashes on the ceiling reflected from the traffic were harsh, their angle steep. Although it was Saturday, I felt I had something pressing to do. The apartment was empty, Christy and Brad had left the *Times* spread on the sofa. As I flipped through, I caught words, headlines, captions. I didn't choose them, they just got pulled into my head.

"Whoa!" I said aloud. The words sounded flat, without resonance, as if I'd spoken on a dry mesa top. I set the paper aside and thought about the final scene of the Brazilian film, the neon van, the traveling players laughing, waving their arms, hugging in the city traffic. I envied them, as I envied my mother and Tony. They didn't need to get to the mine, looking for it was enough.

The phone rang.

"Roxy?" It was my mother.

"Hi."

"You saw the article in the *Free Press?*"

I made an effort to turn back. "Yes."

In spite of her penchant for talk, my mother gets down to business on the phone. She rarely stays on longer than needed to give or receive the message she wants.

"I didn't expect anyone there." She spoke fast. "It was a rough climb and what I needed was to keep still." Then, as if reacting to her own words, she went on more slowly. "They

100

were nice people, we rappelled down the east buttress together, and they drove me back to my car. I didn't know one
of them was a reporter."

I couldn't think what to say. "What did Dad say?"

"He said, 'I'm glad you made it, Bel.'"

"It was a crazy thing to do. You could have been killed,
for heaven's sake."

"You'd rather I hadn't?"

"Yes." I stared at the pigeon droppings on the window sill.

"Your friend Brad called. He wanted to do an interview,
but I told him no, I didn't want to."

"Why?"

My mother was quiet, I shifted the phone against my ear.

"I got scared on the mountain," she said. I could feel her
reaching for the right word. "I was doing fine, plenty of
holds, good rock, it's solid basalt, then for a moment my
mind strayed. I thought: I'm doing this to know what Tony
knows. And I looked down. It took every ounce of force in
me to cover that last pitch."

Below, cars collected behind the invisible dam of a red
light; kids and women with strollers waited on the corner.

"I was mistaken, Roxy. That wasn't a good reason to
climb La Torre."

I let out my breath as if in a dream I had escaped an
enormous danger.

"What are you doing this weekend?" Her question was
so unexpected I could answer calmly.

"I started to break into *Guinness's* with moviegoing, but
quit." The traffic started to flow again.

"Oh?"

"It wasn't what I wanted, to watch things happen. Then a
guy reached over and squeezed my breast. I wasn't even
scared, I just yelled at him. It's dangerous not to feel something like that." A pigeon coasted past the window. "But the
last movie was amazing; it let me see around corners. After
that, there was no reason to go on."

The pause was so long I wondered if I should have said that.

"It's good to know when you're given a gift," she said.

I watched a yellow cab pull up to the curb and a woman
get in. Over the park to the north, hardly noticeable against the
heat-leached sky, pink thunderheads piled up like mountains.

"Yes," I said.

The cab moved back into the traffic.

"You all right, Roxy?"

"I'm fine."

I put the receiver down; my body seemed to lighten and expand. I looked over at the bronze puppy and thought about the lines on its feet, the careful etching of the hairs between its toes. It was a nice thing to know.

Survivors

This isn't my story, but I can tell it better than either Jake or Sam. Their versions are skewed by what they want and don't want to remember, by what they cannot forget. I don't claim to be free of investment in how the story is told or how the events might have changed any of our lives, but I'd like to try to get the facts down straight.

There was no moment of impact for me. The first I knew was the phone ringing at 5:30 on a March morning. It broke me from a dreamless sleep. In the dark, an operator with a singsong accent asked if I would accept a collect call from Jake in Charlotte Amalie, Virgin Islands.

"It's me. Jake," he said. "We're all right, Sam is all right."

I hadn't heard his voice in almost a year; it sounded high and thin, as if he were speaking in an open space and was afraid I wouldn't be able to hear.

"What do you mean, *all right?*" I sat up and shifted my grip on the phone.

"We've had an extraordinary experience, Sam and I. We spent all night in the sea and were rescued a few hours ago."

"The sea?"

"Our plane went down; we were eight hours in the water, eight hours until a tug rescued us."

Jake spoke with the same excitement as he had five years ago when he told me how Sam pitched a close-out game against South High.

"Where are you?

"At the hospital. They brought us here when the boat docked. The doctor's gone over us; we're fine. Sound as a teenager, he said I was." That would please Jake. He keeps himself taut, wiry; he's the same weight as when we were married twenty-five years ago.

"And Sam?"

"Fine. Full of coffee and Cutty Sark." He'd be looking at Sam, I thought, not smiling, keeping it to himself, the way he used to when Sam was little. I settled the quilt around my shoulders; it was cold and rain pecked at the window. I couldn't take hold of what he was saying, but knew I had to ask. "What happened?"

"Here, Sam will tell you." The close hum that connected us ceased suddenly as he passed the phone to Sam. It was too late to say: You're both alive, that's what matters.

"Mom." Sam always spoke my name as a statement. I was a reality; I was there, a person he knew.

"Are you all right?"

"A little drunk, a little wired, but OK."

"And your father?"

"He's amazing. Coughing still, but the doc says his lungs are clear."

I thought of Sam and Jake sitting on the examining table with towels wrapped around them, Sam's chest still smooth, Jake's tanned and matted with grizzled grey hair.

"What are you wearing?"

"Jeans and a T-shirt; Dad's pants are too big, his shirt says Caracas, Venezuela, with a palm tree. The sailors gave them to us."

Outside, grey light showed behind bare trees, rain spilled down the glass. "OK," I said, "tell me what happened." Sam would tell the story from the beginning with plenty of details, the way he'd tell about a movie.

"From San Juan?"

"Yes."

I won't try for Sam's words. Once he spoke them, once I heard them, they were no longer his. I took them in and made them mine.

He didn't much want to go to St. Thomas, but Jake had run out of wine, good wine. You can buy wine in San Juan, but it's expensive, and St. Thomas is a free port. Besides, Jake wanted to show Sam the place. It's a short flight on one of the old World War II flying boats. They got there at noon and had lunch at a seafood restaurant Jake knows and spent the afternoon shopping. Kmart-sur-Mer, Sam called it, only classier. They loaded a couple of cases of stuff on the small plane. It carried only ten passengers, and the pilot was right there where you could see the dials.

About ten minutes into the flight, the plane started easing down. A man across the aisle said the propeller on his side wasn't working. They came closer and closer to the water; Sam knew a plane should be able to fly on one engine, and the pilot hadn't said anything about seat belts. Then the plane hit the top of a wave and bounced up, a wing caught, and the thing flipped. He was upside down, for a minute there, grabbing at the buckle; then he said, "Stop!" to himself and looked down. There was a button release.

The main hatch burst open with bright water beyond, and Jake, already outside, shouted to get lifejackets. The passengers were oddly quiet as they scrabbled toward the opening. One old black man stood in the doorway and wouldn't leave; he couldn't swim. Sam pulled the tab on his jacket and told him to jump. As the last person left, Jake yelled to get the hell away fast. Sam swam a few strokes toward him and turned. The plane, on its back, tilted up slowly like a whale sounding and slid under the waves. It was amazing. Suddenly the bulk of it was gone, and there was nothing.

I thought of them—Sam, Jake, and the others in the terrible emptiness of the sea. Sam wanted to stay with the others, but Jake pointed to a pontoon that had broken off, and they lit out for it swimming fast. After a while, they realized it was blowing before the wind faster than they could swim. Sam said they'd have a better chance with the others. Jake wanted to go on; the others were a good way back, and the wind would be against them.

An island lay on the horizon like a cloud bank. You can't tell distance in the sea. Jake said it was only a mile; Sam was sure it was more. I know the power of Jake's certainty; I've given over to it often enough.

They each hooked an arm through the single life vest and started swimming. Help would come soon. It was late afternoon; low sun raked the waves, and shadows darkened the troughs. After a while, a plane circled behind them where they had gone down, then flew directly over them and dipped its wing. A small fishing boat they'd not seen on the horizon started toward them, but light was going fast as it does in the tropics—the sun drops down and it's night. They shouted and waved; the boat veered off, and the sound of its motor drew away.

I thought of them alone, the close suck and rustle of water, the shifting edge of sky, light drawing in. The picture
was clear, but I felt nothing; my body registered no press of
fear, nothing.

Were they cold? Not at first, Sam said, but were losing
heat to the water all the time. He kept on his shorts and shirt.

"Then I thought about sharks," Sam said. At first he
kicked to keep his feet near the surface, but recognized the
energy it took. "You get wise," he said. He stopped thinking
about sharks. I know the effort of willing, the nights I lay
awake trying to rid my thoughts of Jake.

They talked in spurts: how far the island was, whether
the plane would come back, what happened to the others. It
was hard swimming, the waves were high. On the crests,
they could see land, then they'd slide down and be sur-
rounded by water. As dark came on, lights began to show on
the island; the stars came out. They passed through patches
of phosphorous, and every stroke stirred strange green light.
Sometimes they'd lie back on the waves as if in a hammock
and watch the sky. I thought of them side by side facing up
and the slow tread of their feet under the water.

Once a helicopter crossed between them and the island,
its beam spread like a bright skirt on the ocean, but they
were well beyond the hem and didn't even hear its motor.
The lights on the island did not seem to get closer. Stars rose
behind its bulk, moving sideways as well as up. Sam realized
that a lateral current was sweeping them past the island. He
didn't say anything; Jake had started to take on water and cough.

Some time later, on the top of a wave, Sam saw the riding
lights of a ship and the flare of a search beam, but it was a
long way off, too far to hope. They swam on. Suddenly in
front of them a wave caught an edge of light. Sam turned;
the boat was close, almost on them. They shouted; the beam
moved faster, back and forth. It found them and held. Then,
Sam said, there was the most incredible sound; the boat gave
a long, deep blast. Someone threw out a life ring; Jake caught
it and handed it to Sam. "Get up there," he said.

Sam was pulled toward blinding light. The side of the
ship reared up like a wall and crashed down. A rope ladder
swung over the side. Sam grabbed it, but didn't know if he

could hold on. Then hands grabbed his arms, hauling him up over the rail. Two sailors led him along the deck to a cabin, but he twisted away and ran back as they dragged Jake over the side.

"God, I couldn't believe it. We stood hugging. He would have fallen if we hadn't been holding each other. The sailors thumped our backs, shook hands, and brought us mugs of coffee. Someone pulled out a bottle of Cutty Sark. We wrapped up in blankets and sat on the edge of the bunk and told them our story."

I could not hold all he said, I couldn't think what to say.

"Is your hair wet?"

"We showered to get the salt off. I'm still thirsty."

I hadn't thought about that. Of course they'd be thirsty.

"Dad wants to say something. You'll call Marty, won't you?"

"I will."

"Talk to you later." Again the close hum broke off and then Jake.

"They told me we can get a flight to San Juan in an hour. I'll call when we're home. Tell Martha I got him back safe."

His voice seemed unreal, far away.

"Tessa? Are you OK?" I felt a dart of surprise. Jake rarely used my name.

"Just stunned."

"It's OK. We're alive, we're fine."

"Thank you," I said. "Thank you." But he'd already hung up.

I put the receiver back in the cradle. It is an old phone, heavy and black; perhaps it had attenuated their voices, or perhaps some resonance had washed away in the waves. My hands were cold. I pulled the quilt closer and waited for a surge of relief or thankfulness or joy, but I felt nothing.

It was almost three years since Jake had left. After the first doubling blow and months of painful anger, I found myself loosed of tensions I hadn't known were there. A kind of stasis settled in; I was satisfied with my teaching and found solace in emptiness. But had I, in the process, lost some essential connection? Their story didn't make sense. I was asleep while they treaded the sea. No flicker of unease or troubled dream had warned me of danger.

Since the day Sam was born nineteen years ago, I had to fight an urge to buffer him from unnamed danger. It wasn't anything I could talk to Jake about, the way we had spoken of how tiny and vulnerable Marty was when she was born. It was as if Jake's hopes for Sam were a threat. He wanted him tough, successful, an athlete. Sam was barely eight when Jake took him to see the Orioles play. Then one night at dinner, he announced he'd signed Sam up with Little League. Sam stared at his father; it was clear he hadn't known. Jake hadn't asked me either. He had no right to sign Sam up without asking him, I'd said. Sam looked at Jake and then at me. Marty watched. It was OK, Sam said, he'd try.

He did, and played well right on to high school. One morning in his sophomore year, as he left for school, Sam stood with books in his arms and told Jake he had quit the team. Jake was furious. He and the coach pressed him, but Sam held firm. After that, Jake was barely civil to Sam.

I wanted coffee. I pulled on a wrapper and scuffed into slippers. In the half dark, Dylan, Sam's old Labrador, woke and stretched at my feet. I rubbed his head. He was subdued, uncertain if this was the beginning of the day or an interruption in the night. I went to the kitchen, and without turning on the lights, opened the backdoor. Dylan stood on the steps looking at me as if I were to blame for the rain, then thumped down the steps into the grey garden. I put the kettle on and sat at the kitchen table watching the blue flame.

I was accustomed to the empty house. Sam had left for college last fall, and Marty has been gone since the year Sam quit baseball. She was a gyroscope for us, and, without her there, things between Jake and Sam had grown taut. A small difference about a newspaper article or who left the mower in the rain would erupt into a raging scene. Or else their silence would press air out of the house. Jake spent more and more time at work. Then he told me his company wanted him to open an office in Puerto Rico, and he was going, but with another woman. Maybe Sam already knew about her. He was angrier than I was when his father left. Later, I heard the young woman had left Jake and felt a wave of satisfaction.

I got up and poured myself some coffee. I needed to hear their story again, hear myself tell it. I dialed Marty's number, and she picked up before the second ring.

"Marty, it's me."

"What's happened?" Had they already spoken to her, or

did she somehow know, as I had not?

"I got a call from Dad."

"What's wrong?" I was glad she didn't know, and I told her Sam's story. I don't think I added much, maybe something about the size of the sea at night. I had this image of them resting on the waves talking the way Jake and I used to talk in bed about the future, only they watched the stars and didn't know if they had a future. I imagined a meteor cutting a bright runnel across the sky. Had Sam said that? I wasn't certain.

"You're going down, aren't you?" Marty said.

That was what I had to do. Why hadn't I thought of it? I reached up and snapped on the overhead light. The kitchen gleamed white as a hospital room.

"Yes, of course."

"Tell the airlines. They'll get you on the next plane. Aunt Mary can take Dylan; I'll call the school."

Marty spoke as if she had already practiced the moves.

A few hours later, I was on the plane. I closed my eyes as we gathered speed, and only after the bump of the wheels retracting did I look out. The land was already dim, and within minutes we were in cloud. As we climbed, the mist brightened and suddenly opened to sun. The seat beside me was empty. I was sorry because I would have liked to tell the story again.

I needed to remember their presence. Jake was easy. I carry a hundred still shots of him in my head. He's changed slowly, but the images have aged with him, and I'm startled when I see an old photograph with his hair still black. But Sam seems different each time he comes home. I made an effort to recall how his hand falls over the arm of a chair, how he stretches his legs, ankles crossed, boots exposing their patterned soles, how he holds his head down slightly as if, in spite of the restless outflow of his limbs, his attention circled inward. I had trouble remembering his face.

Two weeks ago, Sam phoned to say that Jake had sent him an open ticket and asked if he'd come to the island over spring break. "I'd planned to go climbing with a couple of friends," he said.

"Think about it," I said. "Do what you want."

Sam hadn't seen Jake in a year. He's as stubborn as his

father, wouldn't take a penny from him for college. He
worked construction in the summers and had an academic
scholarship and a student loan. When Sam called a few days
later to say he was going, I was pleased. Perhaps they would
learn to talk with each other again. Jake had never been easy
with Sam the way he was with Marty. He didn't know how
to talk about Sam, either. When I would try, he'd clam up or
change the subject.

Outside, the cloud cover had broken up; the navy blue
sea was scarred by a single ship the size of a rice grain. I
tried to think of being alone in that huge space. As the plane
began its descent, the sea lightened to aquamarine, flecks of
white appeared and melted, then the island slid from under
the wing much closer than I expected. We swept over bright
cane fields and close-packed shanties around a lagoon,
down to the runway edged with palm trees.

I was startled by the hot thick air and the sharp sound
of Spanish voices. As I'd brought only a carry on, I went
straight to the taxi rank. The cab was old, its upholstery torn,
an advertisement for a night club peeling from the door. The
driver spoke in English, and after I gave the address, I asked
if he had heard of an air crash. Yes, terrible, ten people on
board, only five were saved. I told him one was my husband
and one was my son. As soon as I said it, I was embarrassed.
Why did I need to do that?

Jake's apartment, on the roof of a building in the old city,
was set back on a terrace with pots of flowers behind a
wrought iron gate. I pushed the buzzer. The brass padlock
that held the chain was heavy and foreign looking. No one
came, and I rang again. The hall door stood open, but I
couldn't see in.

"Jake. Sam." My voice sounded stiff, strange.

They came onto the terrace stretching like bears, naked
except for white undershorts, their bodies clean and gleaming. Jake reached through the gate and touched my face, but
before I could take his hand, he pulled it back. I watched
him fit the key into the padlock. His fingers moved with a
familiar awkwardness as if to avoid bending. It isn't age;
he's always moved like that. I glanced away feeling I had
caught him in some private act. When he hugged me, his
skin was cool and had no smell as if some essence had

washed off in the sea. Sam put one arm around me and slung the other over Jake's shoulder as easily as he would over the back of a sofa. He had barely touched Jake in years.

"God, I'm glad you're here," Sam said. Jake's hand tightened on my arm, then he made a fist and tapped Sam's shoulder. I stepped back and looked them over like animals. Sam had scratches across his chest; Jake had an abrasion rimmed with antiseptic on his knee.

"This calls for a drink," Jake said.

Sam watched him go through the door. I couldn't see his face, but wondered if it registered the flick of fear I used to see when Jake said that word.

"He deserves this one," Sam said. I made a gesture to go in to help.

"It's OK, Mom. When Marty called to say you were coming, he got everything ready. He wanted you here."

Jake leaned from the door. "I'm going to get dressed for this important company," he said.

I sat in a rattan chair. Sam walked to the balcony rail, his eyes thoughtful but without the bruised look they often had in Jake's presence.

"He was tough," Sam said. "He thought we were going to die. I was sure we'd make it. It was only when I saw the stars slipping behind the island and Dad began coughing, that I thought, this is it. I was angry. Why the hell had we gone? Booze? Some damned restaurant? Dad's a stubborn bastard. He made us leave the others because he was afraid they'd drown us. We could have gone back. I kept thinking about the guy who couldn't swim.

"We went through a bunch of phosphorous, and Dad ran his fingers through it like it was flowers or something. He was crazy; I wanted to hit him. God, I was filled with this weight, this fury. Then he splashed me, and the phosphorous exploded. Remember how he'd roughhouse when I was a kid? Now we were the same size, and he couldn't hurt me. I could have swum away, but instead I said, hey, we got to move. When he didn't answer, I knew he'd given up. It was like he'd betrayed me again. I spun on him: If you don't think we'll make it, goddammit, I'll go alone. 'We'll make it,' he said. I didn't try to figure if he was lying, but he started swimming again, slow, the way you do when you're in for a long pull." Sam had his eyes on the empty doorway.

He was right not to wonder whether Jake meant it. It takes energy to think about Jake. For years, I wondered what Jake felt about his life, our marriage, me. Maybe nothing, maybe despair. He'd go off and come home from work, as Sam said, the long pull. Maybe he saw no end to it.

The sound of traffic rose from the street, and across the way, bright pink geraniums spilled from a balcony like a tossed negligee. Between the buildings, I could see a swag of sea. Sam turned and stretched. "The whole thing seems unreal, as if it was a story we tell."

"It's not a story," I said. "It happened." I didn't want this to fade into another chapter of family history. That's why I was there, to hear them tell it. Words can fossilize an event before it is used; this was too important to become a story yet. I needed to hold it in my hand like a stone, feel its heft, know it whole, and understand how it connected with our lives.

Jake came through the door carrying glasses on a tray. He'd hung a sliced lemon on the rim of each glass.

"Dom Q's best," he said.

Sam cleared the low table of books and papers. He was taller than his father, but it wasn't size that made Jake seem frail when they were together. Sam gave his attention to Jake as if he had become guardian of his father's dignity.

Inside the apartment, the phone rang.

"It'll be Martha," Jake said. "Sam was asleep when she called."

"I'll get it." We watched Sam cross into the hall. "Mart." He lifted his head and nodded toward us, then looped the wire and moved out of sight.

Low sun washed over the walls. It was pretty light and gave substance to the distance between buildings, between the wall and the potted plants, between me and Jake. He still faced the door.

"He's alive, Tessa." He said my name again.

I reached out and took his hand and pressed his palm to my face. I touched his skin lightly with my tongue. The taste of salt opened in my mouth with a faint residue of bitterness.

"And so are you." I dropped his hand.

"I had this image in my head the whole time—Sam on the beach above the reach of waves. I was afraid the others would turn to him, panic, and pull him under. Later I thought I'd slip my arm out and let him have the life jacket. I thought of him alone; it's damned lonely in the sea." Jake looked down at his hands as if they weren't connected to him. "The sea wasn't against us, just indifferent, profoundly indifferent."

He was silent for a bit. "Mart said a funny thing when I told her; she said it must be a terrible responsibility to be saved." Jake looked at me as if I could clarify what she meant, but that's something he and Sam would have to make sense of for themselves.

Sam came out with a bottle of beer in his hand. "She sends her love." He sat across the table from Jake and looked past him to the narrow line of sea. "You know, when we were swimming, I'd get these ideas," he said. "They weren't really ideas, more like flashes, flicks of strobe light. What I'd leave behind would not be me, only an idea of me, what people would carry in their heads. Like that picture on your desk in there, Dad. It's not Marty, it's a picture of a kid holding onto a horse, yelling to get down."

"She's laughing." Jake spoke quickly. "She wants the horse to trot. I took the picture."

Sam leaned his elbows on his knees.

"See, that's what I mean. I thought she wanted to get off, but that wasn't it. She wanted to go faster. I'm glad that's how it was."

Sam and Jake, their heads thrust forward, the line of their chins level, held as if startled by their own image in a mirror. Jake moved first. He brushed his hand through his hair and reached for his glass.

"We haven't told your mother everything," he said.

Jake began with the reasons for going. He always has reasons, more than he needs. He told how he had to get supplies, how Sam deserved a good meal. They told their tale again, each adding details the other left out.

"When the ship came up behind us, Sam grabbed the vest and waved it. He rose out of the water so high I could see phosphorous caught in the hair around his navel. 'We're here, you blind bastards, we're here!' That's what you said, Sam."

Sam took up the story. Jake bent forward and watched Sam tell the end. I caught the familiar smell of Jake's sweat; I couldn't see his eyes, but their dark centers would have almost obliterated the blue.

"I broke away from the sailors and ran back as they pulled you over the rail."

I was crying now, loose easy tears for a satisfactory ending. But inside me something dry and harsh drew into itself. My story. They would tell theirs over and over. They would hear themselves say they shared a life vest, stars, and talk of dying. I would hear it and know the story didn't make sense. Nothing they had done had saved them, but they came through, and I was here to witness their return.

We sat on the terrace around the table in silence. Light leached from the sky, buildings and flowers lost color, and I felt a huge and dangerous presence had disappeared.

Etcetera Period

I was waiting for the crosstown bus on the corner of Eighty-sixth and Fifth, headed for my Saturday class. It's a cold corner, especially on a windy November day; the sun on my back felt good. Across the avenue, bare trees swayed, and as the traffic flicked past, I caught glimpses between the cars of the rusticated stone wall that keeps Central Park from spilling onto the sidewalk. For an instant, I thought I saw a slit of blue as though a chink had opened between the blocks, and I was looking through to a hot summer sky, like sky over Greece. A truck stopped, blocking my view, and when it pulled away, I could see the stones fitted together tightly with no cracks; the slit I had imagined was below the level of the earth behind the wall.

A bus lumbered to the curb, and I felt for the token in my jacket pocket. My husband, Nelson, buys them by the roll and keeps them in a bowl on his dresser. Every morning on my way out, I take two. My fingers found a split in the lining of my pocket, but it was too small yet to let a dime through. The bus wasn't crowded, and I chose a seat in the rear opposite an advertisement that showed an open window with curtains blowing through. At first, I thought it was an ad for a horror movie, but when I read the text, it was for a burglar alarm system.

I thought of the rift in the wall and the clear hot sky. I wondered where the trees' roots were when they reached the stone barrier. Did they bunch up behind it? I'd have to go back to check the land's slope, see where the water runs off. Since I took geology in college, I notice things like that. The course fulfilled a science requirement, but I liked learning about rocks; they're always there under my feet even if I can't see them. I went on to take mineralogy where we looked at thin slices of rock with polarized light; we learned to recognize each element by its own pattern of line and color. Every pebble has hidden structures that determine how it weathers or how it fractures when it's broken by another stone. Even hills and valleys are shaped in part by the crystals they are made from. Rocks let you know something about a place. I would have gone on with geology, but it seemed too easy, so I majored in history instead.

Nelson used to laugh at my "penchant for stones"; once he bought me a fossil fish embedded in shale that I still have on my desk. But last week he yelled at me, said I preferred rocks to words. He was sore because I'd thrown out a *New Yorker* movie review he gave me to read. He's trying to educate me in the critical language of film. Every couple of weeks, we go to the movies with the Paukers and afterward have dinner and talk about it. I like movies but get bogged down in what to say about them. Reviews seem to tangle people and events with so many words that they lose sight of what happens.

Sometimes I think Nelson uses words to keep himself from knowing things. When he talks about our being "child-free" or making an "alternative choice," I don't know what he sees in his head. In mine, there is a valley of rock without grass, a silent place where nothing grows, nothing erodes. I tried to tell him this once when we were walking in the park, but he held my hand tight and talked about jogging.

He encouraged me to take this Saturday class and so did the school where I teach fourth grade. The current theory is that teachers should know their material in-depth, and the school pays us to take enrichment courses. I'm pretty compliant about these things; I get papers back promptly, change the bulletin board every two weeks, and return parents' calls. I look good enough, and I have learned to keep questions to myself.

When I was little, I once asked a teacher what infinity was. It's a hard idea for a kid to get. I mean, what *is* at the end? There has to be something. The teacher kept saying it curves back on itself. Then what's outside? Finally, she said, "It ends where it began and starts over, etcetera period." The bell rang, and I didn't ask again, but didn't stop wondering. It seems what kids need to learn about is being mystified.

Last week, I filled in for a seventh grade math teacher. I'd lost the copy of the test I was supposed to give, but had the answers on a separate sheet. I wrote them on the blackboard, answers like: it took seventeen minutes for the tub to fill. I told the kids to write questions to fit the answers. They really got into it. They wrote stories where the answers were the punch lines. The next day, the regular teacher was sore because the kids brought in more stories than the teacher wanted to read.

The bus jolted to a stop at West End Avenue where I got off. We have this class at the professor's apartment. Only ten students signed up, and at the first session everyone agreed to meet at his place. They think it's cool being on the in with a writer; I think the guy just didn't want to ride the subway downtown on a Saturday. He teaches English but considers himself "primarily a writer." He calls the course, Structure (?): Function (?) in Contemporary Art. Nelson thought it would be great. "Deconstruction," he said. "You'll outtalk all of us, honey."

We were doing a story that day. Each week we take a different art form—a painting, a play, a movie—and apply a formula for identifying stated and implied levels of meaning, then we pull the thing apart. I'd read the story the night before, transformation theme or cycles or something. It was about two macho anthropologists who find these mounds, "hauntingly beautiful shapes," half-buried in the desert. They hire a local tribesman to help uncover the mounds. He knows the mounds are really abandoned menarche huts for young girls, and it is taboo for men to enter. In order to keep his job, he makes up a story about their being shrines inhabited by powerful spirits. He says he can only dig the sand away on the outside. When the anthropologists go inside, they find remarkably graceful totems of polished wood in the form of animal parts; the language is clever, full of double entendres supposed to make you laugh and feel superior. The anthropologists wonder about the function of the totems; they keep handling them, stroking them. Then they notice changes in their arms, their voices; they recognize the familiar shape of the mounds. It got me riled.

This professor lives in a building that has a refectory table and mirrors in the lobby, but they are dusty, and the elevator man who doubles as janitor is usually grumpy. Everyone was already sitting around the living room. The place

117

was piled with books and journals, the sofa was the kind you buy in a college dorm from someone who is leaving and then cover with an Indian spread to hide the stains. This one didn't have a spread. One woman had brought a cake, so we spent fifteen minutes licking our fingers, brushing crumbs, and calling our teacher David. He told us to call him that; I don't call him anything.

When we started to discuss the story, people tried to be witty, making puns, saying what fun the writer was having with the language, teasing the reader. The class seemed to go on forever, and afterward I was relieved to be outside again breathing air. The woman who brought the cake came out with me. She was desolate because she had to go on to her nephew's bar mitzvah and couldn't stick around to chat informally with David.

I turned down Broadway to get away from her and then onto a side street to be sure. Wind blew dust and bits of paper in a spiral across the sidewalk. A young boy was throwing a ball against an abandoned building; its windows had been broken out of their frames, the door boarded over. The ball hit and bounced back a bit slower on the return, then he'd throw it again. A nice rhythm—arm's lift, arc forward, release, then a step back for the catch. I hoped the ball would go through one of the empty windows, maybe out the other side, that it would pick up speed and head for infinity. If the boy knew, he'd aim for the blank opening and send the ball where it would answer to another gravity. He was so intent on the ball, he did not see me pass.

One in-service training day, the school psychologist lectured about evaluating learning. He said we had to ask what learning looked like. Well, it looks like that boy or kids bursting out of doors leaping into the air, spilling energy over the playground. But the lecturer's answer was something about demonstrating the capacity to manipulate abstractions or showing tolerance for ambiguity, etcetera period.

I remembered a time I learned something. I was thirteen, in a new school and wanting to be part of the in clique. One day in the bathroom, I said mean things about a girl who had befriended me in my first weeks. As soon as the words were out, I realized she might be in one of the stalls. I waited until everyone left, and when she wasn't there, my relief made me feel worse, ashamed on a whole different level, a strata that plunged down under everything I had known before. When I looked in the mirror, I didn't recognize myself.

I made myself stop at the next shop window, not to see the faded oriental rugs or the silver security tape, but to study the surface, my own face. I looked at my grey eyes and suddenly was glad I'd been ashamed, glad I'd been angry in a class. Wind flicked my hair, dust pricked against my ankles. I was standing on a single slab of pink granite, the kind you find sometimes in parts of the city that haven't been rebuilt. It was coarse-grained with big feldspar crystals interspersed with flecks of hornblende and white quartz. I leaned over and ran my finger along the surface. It was dirty, of course, but lovely, hard. Fine striations ribbed the crystals, and bits of mica glinted in the sun.

I stood up and looked at my watch. In twenty minutes, I was to meet Nelson and the Paukers at the Little Carnegie; instead I turned and crossed the street to a phone booth. Its paint had names and numbers scratched into the surface. Nelson was annoyed at my call; he was trying to finish a brief. I didn't make an excuse, just said I wasn't going to the movies or to dinner; I'd see him later at home. He was quiet for a moment. "Are you feeling sick?" he asked. The lift in his voice made me realize he hadn't given up.

"No." I pulled my arm across my belly. "No, I'm fine."

"Then why aren't you coming? I'm running late; there'll be no one to meet the Paukers."

"I'll see you at home," I said and hung up.

I leaned against the booth with my eyes closed letting the image of Nelson's face fade. I recalled how he squeezed my hand in the park until it almost hurt while he talked about jogging.

There are names for things I had forgotten, like the molten mass that presses up from deep in the earth. I had forgotten what force starts it moving, what happens on the surface. I picked up my canvas bag and turned. I would go to the Museum of Natural History, walk up the wide stairway to the geology hall. There would be a model showing how rocks form, how pressure and erosion change them, diagrams showing movements inside the earth. When the place closed, I'd take the crosstown bus and get off by the retaining wall. Maybe in the dark I would glimpse a constellation there that doesn't show on this side.

Bonsai

They had almost finished sorting. Paulie watched her sister shake out and refold a linen tablecloth without paying attention to the direction of the creases. Elizabeth handed her the cloth, then set the stepladder to empty out the top drawer of the highboy. In spite of the fact that Paulie was taller, Elizabeth was the one who usually carried boxes or moved tables. Paulie set the cloth on top of a carton filled with sheets and a pile of napkins embroidered with her mother's initials. She leaned against the wall. "We still have the greenhouse."

"Ma did it," Elizabeth said. "She sent the plants to the hospital. I drove her precious bonsai down in my van; she didn't trust the movers. There's nothing in the greenhouse you'd want."

Paulie hadn't been able to help when their mother packed up. She had already planned to go with Jimmy to the underwriters' conference in New Orleans when Ma sprung the news of her move. Ma had said not to change her plans.

"Some of those pots are valuable," Paulie said.

"But do you want them?"

"Oh, forget it." Paulie taped the flaps of the carton and marked it with her name. "You never liked the bonsai."

"Gave me the creeps the way she'd snip them back and bend the new growth the way she wanted."

"Bonsai is about harmony, is what she told me."

"More like keeping things in their place." Elizabeth closed the drawer of the highboy and backed down the ladder. Paulie watched her carry a rolled up rug out to her van. Elizabeth hadn't taken many things, mostly books, but then she had no kids, and her studio didn't have much living space. When she moved back East last fall after Pop got sick, Elizabeth rented a loft in an old factory. Paulie had stopped by on one of her weekly visits to their parents. The place was huge and drafty. At one end, Elizabeth had arranged a futon, a couple of secondhand chairs, and a table; the rest of the space was her studio. Canvasses leaned against the walls, huge paintings of things—shoes, a half-peeled orange, a bed someone had just left with a magazine face down on it, a crumpled cigarette packet the size of a newspaper. Paulie felt like an intruder, as if she'd entered another world. Nothing was familiar, even a painting of their father's leather chair seemed distorted, the red appearing dangerous.

Since early morning, they had been going over the stuff Ma had left behind, and when Paulie stepped out onto the front stoop, she remembered it was spring. The air smelled of damp earth, the big maple unfolded its first pale leaves, and daffodils bent over the brick walk. As Paulie locked the front door, she ran her fingers across the brass knocker shaped like a shield. It had not been polished in some time. She lifted the knob and let it fall.

"I can't believe she's gone," she said.

"Now there's nowhere to come back to." Elizabeth pushed her hands into her jacket pockets.

"You never did come back."

"No, but the idea I could was always there, always a fall-back." She turned abruptly and started down the walk. "I didn't think I'd care, but I do." She slid open the door of the van for Paulie and went around to the other side.

The night before, their mother had called and asked them to come see her when they'd finished in the house; she had something to tell them. "I hope it's not another surprise," Paulie said.

Two months ago, their mother had shown them her new apartment. It had been her birthday, and Paulie had suggested they take her out to lunch, perhaps the terrace at Le Jardin, but Ma had insisted on driving them herself, said there was a place she'd like to show them. She took them through parts of town unfamiliar to Paulie, rows of houses with white steps and treeless playgrounds. Toward the harbor, Paulie caught flashes of water between the old warehouses, some covered with scaffolding, that lined the waterfront. Ma navigated the narrow streets efficiently, weaving past cement trucks and construction workers unloading lumber.

She pulled up by a renovated brick building that didn't look as if it had a restaurant, but she seemed to know where she was going. Passing through the lobby, Ma nodded to a woman behind the desk; in the elevator, they watched her take a key from her purse. She led them down a corridor, unlocked a door, and stood back with her arm held out. They stepped into a huge empty room. Sun sloped through floor-to-ceiling windows that opened onto a balcony, and beyond the harbor spread out in a wide curve.

"I've already made a deposit on it," Ma said. "Your father's insurance money."

Paulie turned to her sister, but Elizabeth was looking at the view. "Terrific," she said, "terrific."

The van rode higher than a car, and the familiar neighborhood streets appeared distant to Paulie; the flagstone pathways, verandahs with wicker chairs, and azaleas massed in full multicolored bloom seemed oddly prim.

"What do you suppose she'll tell us?"

"She's going to join the Peace Corps."

"Come on, Liz, what do you think?"

"Marriage?"

"It's only six months."

Elizabeth was smiling.

"Who does she know down there by the harbor?" Paulie asked.

"She was having coffee with someone when I left off the bonsai."

"A neighbor?"

"He seemed nice."

"A man?"

"He was helping with the bookshelves."

"Oh, a handyman."

Elizabeth shook her head. "He was pretty good with a hammer."

"You know what I mean."

"Look, Ma is fine. She's made her move; she's fine."

The new apartment already had Ma's stamp—the Bokhara rug, Pop's red leather chair, the bronze figure of a crouching lion. Perhaps it was the light or the white walls that gave a feel of space around each object, or maybe there were fewer things. Ma had left behind most of the pictures and Grandma's collection of samplers.

On a low table by the window was the delicate Izo spruce in a shallow unglazed pot. Paulie imagined her mother placing it there—she'd stand back, shift it off center, check again before she was satisfied. Their house had had bonsai since Paulie could remember—in the hallway, on the dining room sideboard, in the living room. Paulie had loved the little trees, and once Ma found her playing with her plastic horses around the base of a willow. Even now, she remembers her mother's face, her mouth. She was never, never to play with the bonsai again.

She never did, but she would watch her mother from the door of the greenhouse. Sometimes Ma talked as she worked, telling Paulie how, with a twist of wire, she would shape the trunk, how the angle of a branch needed to be brought closer to the ground. Paulie wasn't particularly interested in the process, but found the time with her mother companionable, something she didn't often have. Ma had learned bonsai from her father who'd learned the craft from an old gardener in Tokyo where he had been stationed after the war. "When Father told me I had an eye for finding a tree's character," Ma had said, "I knew I would inherit the bonsai." She spoke of harmony, balance. "Bonsai belongs to the generations." When Paulie had asked what that meant, Ma had told her she was too busy to know yet, but someday she would.

Paulie brushed her hand lightly across the top of the spruce as she might touch her daughter's hair. Harmony and balance. She was a long way from either.

"I don't have chairs for the balcony yet." Ma carried in a tray with a pitcher of wine cooler and long glasses. "We can sit here."

The sofa faced the harbor, but Paulie chose a blue swivel chair by the window. When her mother bought it shortly after the funeral, Paulie had thought it odd, but now saw it was perfect here; you could turn in or out toward the view.

Elizabeth picked up a catalog from the sofa.

"REI. You planning a camping trip?"

Ma, pouring out the cooler, hesitated an instant, then

finished handing around the glasses. She lifted her feet onto the sofa and crossed her ankles.

"As a matter of fact, I am," she said. "I'm going to Alaska."

"Alaska?" Paulie swung to face her. "You mean Elderhostel? A cruise?"

"No, we're driving."

"We?"

"I'm going with Will. Will Turnbull. You met him last week, Elizabeth, when you brought up the bonsai."

Elizabeth was nodding the way she did the day Ma first showed them the place. Paulie felt protest collect in her throat, but couldn't find words. No one spoke. Paulie looked from her mother to her sister with the strange sense that she had been through this scene before. She realized she had, many times. She was the one designated to point out pitfalls, dangers. Elizabeth would stand on the ridge ready to jump into the creek and wait for her sister to remonstrate; she'd wave a lit joint, daring Paulie to try. Suddenly wary of shaping objections, Paulie let space collect around her mother's statement; she set her glass on the center of the coaster. Elizabeth and Ma waited; Paulie let the silence be. A gull sailed past the window; a tanker moored by a warehouse released a plume of dark smoke.

"OK," Elizabeth said to her mother, "tell us."

Ma leaned back on the sofa. "Will's been planning this; he told me about it the first day we met. He came over with a thermos of coffee and donuts after the movers left, said he was a retired harbor pilot, no one could take a berth here without his welcome. The next day, he stopped by again to help with the books, and we went out to dinner afterward. He knows this area, places he and his pilot friends would go for a drink after work."

Ma refilled Elizabeth's glass.

"One of his friends works out of Valdez for an oil company and has been after Will to visit Alaska. He decided now was the time. He bought a secondhand pickup and fixed a camper on the bed with everything he needs. Last week, he asked if I'd go with him, and I said yes."

Ma glanced at Paulie and then Elizabeth. Elizabeth's smile held, but her eyes had tightened to dark blue, the way they did when she would tease or grow stubborn.

"Look. Doc Braun says I'm as fit as a pumpkin. It's not a hard trip. We drive through Canada. We'll camp, check into a motel when we need hot water."

Paulie couldn't believe her mother was saying this.

Ma pointed to the catalog. "That's the tent. We're making a trial run to Chincoteague this week to test the equipment." She spoke as if it were the most natural thing in the world to go off in a camper with a stranger.

Paulie traced the beveled edge of the table with her thumb.

Elizabeth snapped through the pages. "Sleeping bag, air mattress." She looked up. "You're really doing this, aren't you?"

"Do you mind?"

"Mind? Why should I mind?" She pushed the catalog into her lap.

It was Elizabeth's sort of move. Paulie remembered the Thanksgiving dinner when Elizabeth announced she was taking off for L.A. to live with a songwriter. Pop never stopped carving the turkey. "Are you sure this is what you need to do?" he asked. Paulie said she was crazy, wrong. Ma shook her head, but asked where they'd live, whether he worked for a studio.

"What'll you do with the apartment?" Paulie moved to neutral ground.

"That's the joy of this place. The door clicks closed, and I'm gone."

"You won't rent it?"

"No."

At least she could come back here if things didn't work out. Paulie watched a tug slowly pull a tanker away from the dock into open water.

"What about the bonsai?" Elizabeth asked.

Ma touched the rim of the bowl beside the sofa. A clump of miniature cypress. Years ago, Paulie had seen her mother lay the original stem sideways in the soil and fasten it down with bent wire. Layering, she called it. After a few months, small green shoots pushed up. Ma had clipped and trimmed them into saplings; now they had filled out into a small forest.

"I've thought about that," she said. "The director of the arboretum would be happy to have them for their collection, but I offer them to you first. They go as a package—trees, books, tools, containers. Don't take them unless you want them. Bonsai isn't just decoration; the trees need tending, watering. You accept them for what they are—growing things."

She rotated the blue glazed bowl a quarter turn the way she would in the greenhouse. She once told Paulie, "You make the tree more fully itself."

Elizabeth got up and walked to the window. The air in the room seemed to thicken, separating the three of them. Paulie thought the lopsided pine outlined against the harbor could be on a hill above a foreign port.

"I don't want them." Elizabeth's voice was level, each word clear. "I just don't want them."

The boat, some distance from the dock now, was stalled. The tug had backed away, and it, too, appeared unmoving

"I used to imagine I'd set them free." Elizabeth spoke without turning. "I'd take them into the woods and dig a hole; the tree would send out new roots, new branches, but it would never be full, never like a real tree."

The tug eased forward, pressing its shaggy prow against the tanker's stern. Suddenly it seemed to dig in; water churned behind it in a fierce roil, and the ship began a slow pivot.

I'll have to take the bonsai, Paulie thought, learn to water and fertilize, to wire branches the way Ma did, to find the tree's character. But how could she know a tree's character when she didn't know her own? She wasn't clear to herself, had no image of where she was going, what the point of her days were. Her mother had the bonsai, Elizabeth her painting. Paulie had her family, but that, too, had lost shape—the children silent at dinner, Tom in ugly T-shirts, and half the time Jimmy late at the office. What did she have beyond the family and twice-a-week tutoring in an inner-city school? She'd tried needlepoint, taken a course in writing and one in Yoga. Always a beginner. Yoga she quit because when she meditated she thought instead about taking curtains to the cleaners or getting the car's oil changed. To stop thinking those things was dangerous.

Elizabeth turned to face Ma. "Why are you doing this?"

"I've been thinking about it since I learned your father's cancer was terminal. Not about Alaska, but about what it would be like to move on." She brushed her finger across her cheek. "He was so damned good about dying, and I was angry. One night I grabbed the book he was reading and threw it across the room. *Lord Jim,* it was. It broke a branch off the trident maple."

Neither Elizabeth nor Paulie moved.

"Toward the end, I'd come home from the hospital at night and go to the greenhouse. It was good there, glass holding off the dark, the smell of growing, the heft of a trowel. The bonsai saw me through; now it's time to move on."

Elizabeth seemed to listen with her whole body. It had always been like this, the two of them with their work, Elizabeth's big, Ma's small.

"They'd die of paint fumes," Elizabeth said. "I'd forget to water them. I have only north light."

Ma held her hands up, palms out. "You don't have to take them."

"You're damned right I don't. A half dozen dwarf trees. My god."

She slid open the door to the balcony, stepped out and pulled it closed behind her, then fished in her pocket for a cigarette. Her fingers curved around the lighted match, screening the flame like a sailor.

Paulie didn't move; she wanted to hold the distance between herself and her mother, to stay an observer. She knew how easily she could be drawn to compliance.

"Come," Ma stood, "you haven't seen the apartment since I settled in."

Her bedroom was airy, even with the Victorian four-poster. She'd covered it with a bright silk patchwork quilt that had been folded in the linen closet for years.

Ma ran her hand across the coverlet. "It was stored too long."

Paulie hadn't realized how cluttered the old house had been; that's what made a difference—the things she'd left behind, Pop's things, family things.

In front of the windows, her mother had arranged several bonsai like a Japanese garden—white gravel between the containers, a few carefully placed stones. On the wall, she'd hung an enormous painting that Paulie hadn't seen before, a bonsai in a shallow red bowl.

"A house present from Elizabeth," Ma said. "A Japanese black pine."

The tree, slightly off center, was set on a rock; its roots spilled out, reaching into mossy soil. One branch curved low over the edge of the container. The needles were painted in quick strokes of black paint, and the grey trunk showed faint spiral lines where copper wire had torqued it. Scars of old prunings stood out like craters on the moon. It was clearly bonsai, and at the same time, it seemed to hold to the side of a mountain, the red streak of unglazed pot a stone outcrop, the trunk twisted by the steady press of wind.

"Why are you going?" Paulie asked.

"It's time, and I'm ready."

"I'm not; Elizabeth isn't."

"I wasn't ready for your father to die."

"But you're ready to go to Alaska."

"I've been years getting ready." Ma studied the tree in the painting. "You cut off a branch, and the tree takes a new shape."

"Why didn't you let it be, let it grow the way it wanted?"

"I'm not sure anymore." She shifted one of the white stones. "I was pleased when my father passed his bonsai to me."

"Now you want one of us to take it."

"No," Ma shook her head slowly. "No. I want you to choose for yourself. I didn't," she said. "I did what he expected me to do."

"That's the way I've lived my life."

"I know you have. But now, in this, you can choose."

Paulie looked out past her mother. "Maybe," she said, "maybe I can."

Beyond the grove of little trees, the harbor stretched toward the far shore—low buildings, cranes, a cluster of gas tanks. The tug, tied now to a nearby wharf, rose and fell with a light swell, and the tanker, already past the narrows, moved out toward open water, toward the sea.

The Three of Them

Passing on Messages

Gladys said she came to talk about the retirement home up near where they live, but that wasn't the real reason; she came to find out about Flag. Mothers and daughters, seems they lose connection. Oh, Gladys brought folders and talked about the place, but she knows full well I'm not going to any home. When I can't carry in the wood, I'll sell a couple of back acres and hire someone to help.

"It'll be perfect," she said. Doesn't she know yet there's no such thing as perfect? After seventy-five years I've learned, although I'm still open to dreaming.

She put me in mind of the salesman who'd come to show Travis catalogs of farm equipment. He'd go on about a new baler or disk harrow, showing pictures of attachments and replacement parts. Later Travis said it was the man's job, they both knew he couldn't afford to buy anything.

We'd had a week of rain before she came, and the grass was ragged. Gladys would notice, but who needs lawn? The flower beds look good. Travis made them for me twenty years ago from tractor tires. Since he died, I give them a new coat of white paint every April; now they were spilling out with nasturtiums, asters, marigolds. All different colors.

Flag and I put in the seeds. We'd gone to the farm co-op, and she'd turned the rack, pulling off the packets with the brightest pictures. She comes by an interest in flowers from her grandfather; it was Travis first called her Flag. Gladys named her Iris, but Travis said her eyes were the color of the wild flag that grows by the pond. The name suited her.

I let Gladys show me pictures of little houses stuck together and attached to a central building. I asked her, "What's it look out on?"

She turned real quick. "What does that matter?"

I didn't answer but nodded out past the barn. Midsummer pushed in on all sides: the near field in clover, beyond a strip of corn almost ready for cutting, then a stand of barley bright green against the sky.

There's nothing mean about Gladys, but she has an idea of how a daughter should be. She calls every week, and when she visits, brings me presents like a heating pad for my shoulder. Once it was a gadget to pick things off the floor that came with this terrible catalog that had pictures of aluminum walkers and wheelchairs and diapers for grown-ups. We may need them, but it got me mad, though maybe scared is more like. Now Flag, she made me one of them metal chimes you hang up; it blows in the wind and gives a deep ringing sound like it comes from far off. Hard to think they're mother and daughter.

You could say the same for me and Gladys. We never hit it off right. She was born full-term, six months after Travis and me was married. An ugly little thing; even the puppy was cuter. I'd think that, then I'd snatch her up and hug her. Travis said he was glad to have a daughter; that's what he wrote on her birth certificate, Gladys. She's a good girl; she tries.

And I'll say this, she always liked animals. Travis brought her rabbits and ducks when she was little, then a horse named Trotter. We thought she might be a vet, but she wanted out of Pine Grove real bad, and when Matthew Waters came to our church straight from the seminary, she set her cap for him. Travis didn't much care for him, but Gladys thought he was a knight. After they married, they lived in the village for a few years. It was a relief when they got the parish up in Scranton; it's hard having a good daughter close to hand. I missed Flag, but later when Gladys got busy having her boys and being Mrs. Reverend, she'd send the child to spend the summers here on the farm.

Now Matthew has this bee in his hair about my moving into the retirement place his church runs. It's no holiday getting old. I nursed Travis's mother for four years, and then Mary Keedy from the next farm. Travis and the boys cut her wood and kept the place mowed; when she took bad, I was over there twice a day. It's not like that now. Wayne Keedy is a good enough neighbor; he farms my fields and plows out my road in winter, but his wife works in town, and their kids are in day care. Things is different. I'll know when the time comes to go somewhere.

After Gladys put away the folders, she finally come to what she was here for and asked about Flag. I told her how the girl had taken up with Jesse Stabler, Tom Stabler's son, and moved into a trailer with him over to Turkey Ridge. After college was out in May, Flag had stopped to spend a week with me, and on her way here, her car lost its muffler. I said to go look for one in Tom's junked car lot.

Flag's a pretty fair welder. In high school, Gladys wanted her to take dressmaking, but Flag signed up for welding instead. Tom's boy, Jesse, showed her round the lot, and she borrowed a welding torch to take a muffler off an old Mustang and put it on hers. At the end of the day, Tom offered her a job. She wasn't anxious to go back to Scranton, so she took it.

Funny how things happen. Flag read about this course on welding in the college catalog and signed up for it. In her high school class, she was good at fine work, but this course wasn't about welding parts, but making sculptures. Flag said you look at things and think about how they balance, then put pieces together like a tractor seat with barbed wire to show how they speak to each other. I had nice pictures in my head of what Flag would make. Esther Wainwright paints real pretty scenes on old saw blades and sells them at Apple Butter Festival. She makes good money at it.

Last week, Flag and Jesse come over one evening with a sculpture for me. It was made from a fancy iron grille shelf she'd taken from our old cookstove. She'd found it in the gully where we used to dump stuff before trash removal and had welded the pieces together to look like a goat. Jesse carried the thing down to the tire flower beds, but Flag made him move it, first one place then another until he set it by the big boulder Travis could never get rid of. Jesse kept looking at me and shaking his head as if she were half crazy, but I could tell he was half crazy for her.

When Gladys left here to visit Flag in the trailer, I don't know just what happened, but Flag called right after her mother left and said she was coming over, she had to talk. She called from Tom's shop; there was a lot of noise in the background, and her voice was tight, the way it sometimes is after a visit from her mother. I wonder, did Gladys feel that way about me?

My mother's been dead fifty years now, but I can still hear her. She was always on to me, telling me "should" or "ought to." Do we ever get rid of that voice? I thought of lines of mothers and daughters going in both directions, passing along messages, and not one of us perfect.

When Flag took up with Jesse, she told me he was fixing a place for her. She watched my face as she went on about how he'd located an old trailer, and his Dad said he could set it up on the far side of the ridge. I don't like them mobile homes. Insubstantial they are. Everything all provided, but tacky. I didn't say.

A couple of weeks later, she took me to see it. Came and drove me there like a real guest. It's off a township road they haven't paved yet. A few farms are still working, but a lot of the fields have gone back to scrub. The country's changing. We turned up a lane running along a hay field toward the ridge. Below the crest, where the land flattens, Jesse had set the trailer. It was low to the ground and painted brown with a stand of pine beside it. A real pretty spot. The clay was still raw, but they'd planted rye, and it was already showing green.

Flag stood back when I got out of the car, "Well?"

I took in the quiet and how the sun drew out the smell of pine pitch. "Nice," I said.

She opened the door to the trailer for me. They had broke out the inside walls to make one big room full of light. The east end was all windows giving over the valley; at the other end was a kitchen with a counter.

"It's not finished yet, the electricity's not in." I noticed a Coleman lantern hanging over the table. "Jesse's going to fix a place outside for me to work. A studio."

They didn't have proper chairs, but seats taken from junked cars. One made of brown leather was heisted onto cinder blocks. "Jesse did that for you, Grams; it's not so far down. He took it out of an old T-bird."

"It's real comfortable."

It was. The whole place was comfortable. I felt a spurt of envy. Starting out. I remember the hopes of beginning. Somehow fixing up a house would make things work. The trick was to get it right.

"Would you like coffee?" Flag had cups ready and a plate

of cake.

"With milk." That's not what makes it right, the cake, the coffee, or even the trailer; it's what's between the two of you.

Flag set the cup on a crate beside my chair, then looked up. "I'm acting like Mom, aren't I?"

"She'd be surprised."

"But not pleased. This isn't the way she'd want it."

"You can't be sure. Your mother didn't have it easy."

Flag turned. "She got what she wanted: a big house, a safe husband, two boys, and a girl that didn't match up."

"She got what comes; it's not the same thing."

"Jesse's not like Dad, all-fired certain about everything. And he thought to make me a place to work."

"Your mother has a sewing room."

Flag flicked her hand as if to brush off a fly.

"We don't all get to choose," I said.

She shook her head. "Stay on my side, Grams."

"It's not sides I'm talking; it's your work I'm thinking of."

"You mean college?"

"Work. You know it when you do it."

We was both quiet for a bit.

"Want to see where Jesse's going to put the studio?"

Outside, she pointed to the slope behind the trailer. "He'll backhoe into the hill and use the fill to grade it level."

"Handy to the house," I said.

The dirt track we'd come by went on up to the top of the ridge. I thought of the view from there. "I'd like to see acrost the valley, back to where the farm is," I said.

"It's a pretty steep walk."

"It's downhill on the way back."

Flag shrugged. It wasn't far, but a stiff slope. I could see sky through the pines like they was a fringe closing off the space beyond. The trees ended at the top, and the road bent down into the next valley. Below us a junkyard spread across the side of the hill like a small city. Rows of rusted cars curved along grassy paths like a tiny housing development, like the pictures Gladys showed me.

"That's some view," I said.

"Tom planted spruce trees so you can't see it from the road."

"Well you can from here."

"They have to be somewhere, besides, it's his living."

I like that in Flag. She's loyal.

"Jesse's going to get a computer. He'll have every car in the lot recorded, and he'll hook in with a nationwide used parts system. It's big business. He showed me an article. 'Hidden Gold,' it was called."

"Rusting iron, more like," I said.

"He has savings set aside."

"For buying a trailer and fixing a place for you?"

"He's getting ready; this is the first step."

"You have two more years of college before you're ready."

Flag looked out over the little city, frowning.

"You pregnant?" I asked.

She brushed her hand across her hair. "Mom asked the same thing," she said. "I know about birth control. I got pills from the clinic at school."

"Well, use them. Don't narrow your choices."

"Mom hasn't liked a single choice I've made."

"Don't be so sure." A pair of crows slid across the trees. "When I first met Travis, he was going to have the best registered holstein herd in the county, a big milking parlor, a new wing on the house. Well, I have them flower beds, and they're still real pretty."

Flag reached over and put her hand on my arm.

"Grandpa gave me my name," she said. "He taught me about tools. Remember the plank bench he helped me build? Mom still has it in front of the fireplace."

"See, she liked that."

Flag's hand tightened. "There's Jesse." A blue pickup wove between the rows of cars. We watched it come up the track and pull in beside us.

"Hey, hey." Jesse leaned over and opened the cab door. "I'll drive you home in style."

Flag gave me a hand up the high step. I pushed aside a tumble of beer cans on the floor.

"Like our place, Grams?"

Jesse reached across me and squeezed Flag's thigh. She turned to him real slow and smiled.

"We're going fishing," he said.

"When?"

"I told Hank Heller we'd meet him at the boat ramp at five. He has a new outboard for the whaler."

I know that Hank Heller. He's down to the Log Cabin Inn every Saturday night, and generally in a fight.

"But we have spare ribs for Grams tonight."

Jesse kept his eyes on the road. "She can come with us fishing, or we can drop her off on the way, and she can come again tomorrow. Hank's only free tonight."

I was suddenly ready to go home and leave them to their squabbles and dreams. I wanted my own house. Flag would do what she was brave enough to do, if only she could see to choose.

I waited in the cab while Jesse set fishing gear and an Igloo chest in the truck bed. Flag slid in beside me with jackets on her lap.

"I'm sorry, Grams."

"It's OK."

"He loves fishing."

They all love fishing.

I was picking dead heads off the marigolds when Flag drove up to the house. She came over and watched me work for a bit, then went to the shed for clippers. She squatted down and went after the orchard grass the mower had missed beside the tires.

"This stuff creeps in everywhere," she said.

The smell of damp earth mixed with the sharp smell of nasturtiums.

Flag spoke without looking up. "Ma had a fit about me and Jesse."

"What did you expect?" I tugged at a dandelion.

"She got kind of crazy, said things I've never heard her say before. Wild, like I'd done something to her."

"Well, haven't you?"

"What do you mean?""

"You never once thought: Gee, Mom would hate this?"

"I didn't choose him for that." She tossed aside a clump of grass. "That was extra."

"Choose? Seems Jesse chose you."

"That makes it better."

"Why?"

"It's good to be wanted."

"And who's satisfied, you or Jesse?"

"What are you getting at, Grams?"

"Want, need. You better learn the difference."

Something made me remember Gladys when Matthew Waters came to ask for her hand in marriage. He was old-fashioned, prissy almost, with his round eager face. Gladys watched him, and I knew in that instant what he wanted of Gladys and that she would give it to him. I hadn't taught her how to know what she needed for herself.

If she didn't know, how could she teach Flag? But she must have sensed something wrong, that's why she talked half crazy. We don't have any way to speak about these matters, to ask the questions. It's not like teaching arithmetic or *Hiawatha* or even telling the truth. It's not written in any book I've read, yet it's as clear as this July day: pay heed to your needs. If I had told Gladys, she could've passed it on to Flag. I can't do Flag any good, she has to hear it from her mother.

"What you want, girl, is something you might get and something you might not. What you need, is to learn to get along with what you have, yourself."

"Mom wouldn't speak when she left. I told her I don't give a fuck."

"That was real friendly," I said. "You go home and do some thinking. I can't do it for you."

I couldn't see her face; she was still clipping the orchard grass. "Jesse's gone off," she said.

"Oh?"

"He went off in a camper with Hank Heller and two other guys this morning. They're after pike upstate somewheres."

"You're always welcome here." I said it before I could stop myself.

She shook her head. "Tom has a big order to fill. He's counting on me."

"Good."

I watched her little car jounce down the hill. It looked out of place on the rough road.

I was in the kitchen culling beans when the phone rang the next day. It was Hank Heller. He couldn't reach Tom, he said, and the trailer has no phone. Jesse was in a car accident and broke his leg. He was in the hospital in Altoona.

As I drove over to find Flag, I was thinking all the while of how she'd manage this. From the road, I could see a shower of sparks where she was welding beside the trailer. It all looked peaceful set there in the pines. She couldn't hear me over the hiss of her torch, and she had on one of them big helmets with a panel of dark glass. I had to step into her line of sight before she looked up and switched off the torch.

She pushed the mask up. "What's wrong?"

"Jesse's had an accident." I told her what I knew.

"That fucking Hank Heller." She took off her big gloves and threw them on the ground. "Where the hell's Altoona?"

I brought a map from the car. "It'll take you a couple of hours anyway."

She turned the gas off at the tank and put her tools in the shed leaning against the trailer.

She looked over at me. "Want to come?" I shook my head. "Right. My work, isn't it?"

I didn't offer to have them in the house even if they was without electric.

When Gladys drove in this morning, I figured she'd come to find out if Flag planned to go back to college, but she didn't even ask about her. She come and picked beans with me and then went for a walk. It wasn't like her; she hasn't stepped off the porch here in years. And afterward she wasn't in a hurry. I made us lunch and told her, thank you, but no, on the home. She nodded but didn't seem much interested, then she asked about Jesse.

I poured us both more coffee. "He's not up to Flag," I said, "but she'll have to find that out for herself."

Gladys has this way of looking at me, wanting something and afraid to ask. It used to drive me crazy, but right then it turned my heart. "What did I do wrong?" she said.

"Same as me."

"What do you mean?"

She watched me with a kind of fierceness. I knew I had to answer.

"Look, Gladys, we both know I wasn't the best mother to you. I didn't want a baby right off like that, didn't give you proper welcome. Thank god for Travis. He was dotty about you. Oh, your brothers too, but you were his best beloved."

"Mama." Gladys looked at me like checking to see if I'd changed shape.

"If you're angry, you've a right, but don't pass it on to

Flag. Your way to cover need was to please, hers is to act ornery. What you're after is the same."

I reached out and touched Gladys on her knee. She put her hand on top of mine hard, as if I was about to pull it away. She was probably right; I wouldn't have left it there long.

"Why didn't you say this before?"

"I was ashamed."

Usually it's Gladys who cries, but this time it was me. I wanted to take her and hug her and tell her I was sorry. But we know each other.

We sat on the porch real quiet for a bit, then Gladys got up. "I should go," she said.

"Say hello to Flag for me."

"I'm not going there, not until she asks me."

"So what's the should?"

She turned and faced me. "You know there isn't any."

The sun was going down red behind the barn. "If I take the back road, maybe I'll catch the sunset a second time from the top of the ridge," she said.

As she went down the path, she swerved over to the goat Flag had made. She ran her fingers down its back the way she used to run her hand down old Trotter's flank, then turned back to the car. She drove off with her hand out the window, not waving, just holding, like Travis used to do when he went off to the cattle market or somewhere he was pleased to go.

Checking on Iris

"How can you be so sure?" Mama said it real sharp, as if it weren't my business.

I said Iris was throwing her life away on that boy. We were sitting at Mama's kitchen table, and I'd spread out the folders Matthew wanted me to show her about the retirement community his church is sponsoring. I knew she wouldn't hear of it, but had been glad for an excuse to come down and check on Iris without seeming to interfere. She sees more of her grandmother than she does of me, but out of the blue she'd sent a letter. I'd had maybe one birthday card during the two years she'd been away at college. The note said she'd moved into a trailer with Tom Stabler's son up on Turkey Ridge. It took the breath out of me. I didn't know what I felt or who I could tell. Not Matthew. I imagined his face turning red, making his hair seem whiter; his eyes would go flat, and he'd close his mouth into a thin line. Funny, it was Mama I wanted to tell, although she generally takes Iris's part.

She was looking at me the way she sometimes does as if she was seeing through me to another person.

"Mama, listen to me," I said. "It's no good. She has to finish college."

"What's *has* to?"

"You always ask that: *who says has to, who says should?* I don't know; I can't see life without it."

"Maybe she's trying to live without *should.*"

Mama's hardheaded, stubborn, and Iris is like her. They're a pair. Mama was never a cozy grandmother the way I imagined she would be. When Iris a baby, Mama used to talk to her as if she was talking to a grown-up friend. One day, I heard her going on in the kitchen; she was paring potatoes at the sink, not even looking at the child. She'd set Iris down on a blanket in the middle of the floor with tin measuring cups to play with and was telling her how she'd found a big old snakeskin stretched over the tops of the preserve jars down in the cellar. She told how the snake grew all milky, even its eyes, until everything was blurred, and it couldn't stand its skin anymore. It would rub against some rough place like the unplaned wood shelves or the zinc lids of mason jars and would wiggle around peeling its skin back, inside out, until it was loose. Then the snake would slide out all black and shining. I came in and scooped Iris off the floor. Stories like that could give the child bad dreams.

"If I talk to her, maybe she'd come home." Even as I said it, I knew it wouldn't work. The girl's been contrary since she was born—a picky eater as a baby, she wouldn't wear the clothes I made her, and when it came to church affairs, she fought at every turn until I was embarrassed to be the pastor's wife. Since she went to college, I don't think she's crossed the threshold of a church except for Pa's funeral service. Now she's living unmarried in a trailer.

Mama was no help. "Do what you have to do," she said.

As she walked with me to the car, she pointed out a jumble of bits and pieces of iron next to the tire flower beds that Iris had welded together. "A sculpture," Mama called it.

Iris doesn't have a phone, but I know where the place is. Jesse's father, Tom Stabler, was the class below me in school, and his family's farm was over on the next ridge. I never had much to do with Tom, but I liked him, a real quiet boy. He quit junior year to join the navy, and they sent him over to Vietnam. I found the road all right, but it looked different, darker, closed in by pine trees. When I turned off to the house, the fields were still there behind the trees, but they were covered with junked cars—rows and rows of them filling the hillside. It was like a slap, coming round the bend and seeing them; I would have turned back if it wasn't for Iris.

No one seemed to be around, but the sound of a motor came from the barn. I got out and walked to the open door. Tom, I was sure it was Tom, was working under the hood of a pickup with the air compressor going. I must have thrown a shadow because he ducked his head out and stared at me a moment, then set down his tools and came toward me squinting into the light. His hair's gone grey, and he has a beard, but no belly like most of the men around here.

"Gladys. I'll be darned."

I had forgotten his smile. It opened like a window onto sky, and I'd forgotten how he looked at you direct, as if he were learning something important.

"Hello, Tom." My voice sounded flat, prim.

"What is it? Twenty, twenty-five years?"

"Something like that."

"Gladys Havermeyer." He shook his head. "Your glasses are new."

Tom used to notice details you never thought about. Once walking out of school together, he said the way I held my books against me was like I was carrying a small wild animal.

"I'll bet you didn't come here looking for Tom Stabler, but for that daughter of yours."

I nodded.

"They're up over the ridge. Jesse's set on getting the old trailer fixed for her." He watched me as he spoke. "She's a real good worker, that girl. Never knew a lady welder before."

"She learned in school. Took welding instead of sewing."

Tom laughed. "Sounds like a girl I knew missed the school basketball championship to tend a sick rabbit."

"And the rabbit died."

I turned back to the car; Tom followed me out and leaned on the window.

"Take the track there through the lot up to where it crosses the ridge. You'll see the place just beyond." He shook his head again. "Good to see you, Gladys. I always figured you'd be one to get out of here. Funny your daughter come back."

He tapped the door, and I pulled away. The track passed through rows of junked vehicles with broken headlights and cracked windshields, one with a big spiderweb where someone's head had hit. I couldn't believe I was here to fetch my daughter. When I come back to Pine Grove, it sometimes feels as if I've never been here before, yet when I drive up to the house with its sagging porch and shabby gingerbread trim, I get this kind of pain. For years, I visited only when I had to. Pa was always pleased and would want to take me to town with him to get the mail, or pick up feed at the co-op, some excuse to show me off. I've lost touch with almost everyone here; my two best friends have married and moved away.

Mama keeps me informed about old classmates—who had a new baby, who was on the church auxiliary, then later, whose daughter was pregnant and had dropped out of school, and sometimes who was on food stamps. It was as if she were reminding me of where I came from. Once when I fetched Iris after she'd been visiting, Mama said, "Don't get too grand up there. Remember your daughter's feet are the wrong size for glass slippers." I never know how to take those things Mama says.

And she's tart about Matthew. She doesn't seem to mind about my brothers, Bobby being president of the Lions over in Waynesboro and Mel with his own electric business. She always remarks on Matthew's big stone church and the rectory as if they were some terrible extravagance. She doesn't know the fancy houses in our part of town were broken up into apartments long ago. People hang laundry on the porch, men without shirts work on cars in their driveways, and you can hear fights on Saturday night.

Matthew is no help with Mama. He was always afraid of her, and since he got involved in the counseling business, he speaks of her with a kind of awe. A few years ago, he went on a retreat for clergy and took this seminar on counseling. He came back with ideas for setting up groups for parishioners: AA, Smokenders, Getting to Know Yourself. At first he gave me books to read, and talked about the inner child. What about the outer husband? I asked him. It made him sore, but he quoted my words in his sermon the next day to show something about duty. He's like that. If he took the boys to a single Little League game in the season, he'd manage to bring it into his talk on Sunday.

Now John is the only one at home, and he's just there to eat and sleep. The house feels closed up. Matthew is around, of course, but always in his study. I can hardly picture in my mind what he looks like across the table; it's as if I saw through hazy plastic, nothing has an edge, nothing is quite in focus. But I can see here clear enough—a junkyard, and I'm looking for my daughter.

Iris didn't know I was coming, but she'd know straight off what I had come to say: *Go back to college. Get yourself a passport to the life you choose.* I thought I had done that when I married Matthew. I thought I chose well, a young minister just out of seminary, but I was afraid to go off on my own. Why else did I come back to Pine Grove as school librarian as soon as I finished college?

Grass brushed the underside of the car, and I wondered if I might hit a hidden rock. From the top of the ridge, I could see the trailer off to the right; the valley beyond stretched out to farms and woodlots and hills that lay blue against the sky. This was Iris's view. The rectory is squeezed between the parish house and a brick apartment building; our garden was taken over as a parking lot for the church ten years ago. I try to keep the flower beds in front looking nice, but kids pick the blooms and throw cans over the iron fence. We don't live the way Mama thinks we do.

I parked between an old Ford pickup and Iris's red car. It's front fender was spray painted a dull grey. The ground beside the trailer was raw clay, a private junkyard it seemed, with canisters of gas, parts of an old stove, and welding equipment stacked beside a worktable.

I called out, "Hello," but everything was silent. How often I seem to call into empty places. Last week I came back to the rectory with the groceries, and it was the same thing. I could hear the TV coming from some room closed off upstairs, but no one answered. When I called again, a long-eared dog came through the open door and barked once without moving, then Iris looked out. "Mom! My god. What are you doing here?" She put her hands on either side of the door.

"You don't have a phone. I came to see Mama and thought while I was there, I'd drop in on you."

"Well, that's . . ." She turned and spoke over her shoulder. "It's Mom. My mother."

"I hope this isn't a bad time."

A young man came up behind her in the doorway. His hair was tied back, and he wore an undershirt without arms.

"Meet Jesse," Iris said. "We're hooking up the gas stove."

As he came out, he wiped his palm on his jeans. I watched myself shake his hand.

"It's a mess inside," Iris said, "we can sit out here."

The dog came over and sniffed me.

"What's her name?"

143

"Bramble."

I stroked her sleek nose and narrow back. "Part hound, I'd guess."

"Bluetick."

Iris unfolded an aluminum strap chair. My skirt was tight, and I had to keep my knees pressed close together so it wouldn't ride up. Iris leaned back in an old car seat propped against the building, her legs stretched in front of her. Jesse brought out two cans of Coke. He handed one to me and one to Iris. She glanced at him and smiled.

"Thanks," she said.

"I better get that pipe wrench before Pop closes up for the day." He went off to the pickup. Iris watched him swing into the cab; her eyes followed the truck until it turned up the hill. She pulled open the tab of her Coke and took a drink. I set mine on the ground.

"I thought you had an internship with the park service this summer," I said.

"I did, but this welding job came along. It's more what I wanted."

"Iris," I said, "how can you?"

"How can I what?"

"This is no place for you, this backwater." I didn't want to talk this way; I shouldn't have come.

"Grams lives here. She has for her whole life."

"That's different. Things have changed. This was farm country then; it's ugly now, rough. People get drunk on Saturday nights. Half the town's on welfare. Playing house doesn't make it right."

"Playing?" Iris straightened. "We live here. Is that playing? Is having a job and my own place, playing?"

"Iris." I pressed my hand against the surge rising in my chest. "Can't you see, choices must be made."

"You made a choice. You married Dad."

"I made a careful choice."

"And you're glad?"

"Your father was a good husband."

"Was?" She bent forward toward me. "You said *was*."

"We're talking about *your* life, not mine." It came out sharper than I meant. "Don't get caught by what looks safe."

"What does that mean?"

144

"Like fixing up a house or living out the story you tell yourself is what you want. Like marriage."

Iris looked at me as if I were saying crazy words. She held still for a moment and then leaned forward.

"I am a sculptor," she said.

"A sculptor?" I felt a small burst like light inside me.

"Is that so terrible?" she said.

I don't know what set me off, but I was crying.

"God, Mom. You think I'm a fallen woman or something?"

I couldn't say anything, just shook my head.

"Because Jesse's father runs a used parts business?"

I got up still shaking my head. Iris leaned back. "I don't give a damn what you think," she said, "it's my life."

I held up my hand so she wouldn't go on and walked to the car. She hadn't heard, hadn't understood.

Iris came up beside the car and put her arm along the open window. She started to say something, but bit her lip and shrugged.

"You don't have to go back through Tom's lot again," she said. "The lane there takes you down to the town road."

I was glad she told me, but didn't try to speak. I nodded and started the car. As I pulled off, her hand slid along the fender.

I'd done this all wrong. Iris was angry for the wrong reasons; Mama considers me a prig; Matthew won't notice I'm gone until no one serves him his dinner. The rip I'd felt had loosed a tumble of confusion; it almost seemed I was the one who was angry.

I didn't take the interstate home, but went instead on back roads that pass through the small towns, farmland, and second-growth woods of the strip-mine country south of Scranton. The hills have odd flat tops with sharp slopes; the trees are more or less the same size, poplar mostly, round silver leaves that quiver in the wind. Occasionally I glimpsed a lake, long and narrow, where water had filled a pit, but mostly just manmade woods.

A flash of pink caught my eye. I slowed the car and backed up. A swathe of bright magenta flowers filled a small dip. I stopped and got out. The blossoms, shaped like shooting stars with fringed centers, pressed through mossy earth. I had never seen the flower before and wondered if it was native to this barren ground.

Before I married and moved to Scranton, I used to know the woods around the farm by heart, where the columbine or lady's slippers grew, but since then I've had no time for wildflowers. I let them go along with a lot of other things. The place was quiet, and I could hear my own breathing. Leaves clicked, a bird called high and far off.

When I told Matthew about Iris and the trailer and Jesse, he kept tapping the magazine he was reading. He didn't want to hear; it skewed the image of his perfect family. Had he ever really looked at Iris, seen her in any light other than the way he wanted her to be? Had I?

In the week that followed, Matthew made no mention of Iris. Nothing was settled, but I had said what I needed to say even if she hadn't heard, and I didn't fret about her. When Mama called to tell me that Jesse had broken his leg, I felt a spill of anger—another hook to hold her. Then I thought, she has to see that herself, she has to decide.

I wanted to talk about Iris, I wanted to talk to Mama. The next day, I drove down and was there by midmorning. She was out in the garden picking beans. I worked along with her but couldn't get myself to speak of Iris, and after a bit I went for a walk. The old lumber track still takes out from the upper corner of the east field, but the woods have changed; the gypsy moths have killed a good number of oaks. Someone had been through with a four wheeler, but grass was already filling in the ruts. I found the spring Pop had showed me years ago. We'd built stonework around it where moss and fern now grew in the crevices. Beside it, a jelly glass hung upside down on a stick; it wasn't the one I had put there, but I was pleased to see it and took a drink. The water was cold and tasted of earth.

Later, Mama and I sat in the kitchen and drank coffee. We talked about her neighbors, how Wayne Keedy from the next farm works her fields and cuts her stove wood, hunting the land in autumn in exchange.

"He's not beyond taking a deer out of season when they get into the wheat. Keeps my freezer in venison."

I still wanted to talk about Iris, but didn't know how to start. It stings my pride that she is easier with Mama than with me, and Mama knows it. Sometimes she teases me with

146

it. But I wanted to know.

"Tell me about Jesse Stabler."

Mama stopped stirring her coffee. "You knew Tom? Well, he's Tom's son. Not a bad boy, but no push. He can't hold a candle to Iris." She set her cup down carefully. "But she has to learn that herself. She has to ask herself if she wants to live with it."

Those were the same words I'd thought.

"Why can't she see?" I said. "What did I do wrong that she can't see?"

Mama was watching my face and kind of drew in as if collecting herself; she started to speak the way you begin a complicated story.

"I wasn't always a good mother to you," she said. She told me I was conceived before she was married. I knew that, but she had never said it before. She told me how Pa took to me from the moment he saw me as if she hoped that would make up for her. She said I'd a right to be angry and hurt; she said things I didn't think she could know, things I hadn't said to myself. Her words broke out so fast, I couldn't hold them all. I thought of calves loosed from a winter pen, how they flare out across the pasture, galloping, bucking, tails high.

Afterward I told her about the flowers I'd found, and we looked them up in her wildflower book. She had come across a stand of the same ones long ago on the far side of the ridge but had never been able to find them again.

Later we sat on the porch with a colander of beans between us and snapped the ends onto spread newspaper. I told her I was afraid Iris wouldn't go back to college.

"Don't be so sure," Mama said. "She's looking for her work."

"Her work?"

Mama nodded toward the sculpture Iris had made by the tire flower beds. I'd not seen it from this distance before. Up close it was made from scraps of iron, parts of the woodstove we used to have in the kitchen, but from here I could see it was shaped into a goat. The head was raised, and the horns swept back, the feet and body collected, ready to leap.

That's how I feel, ready to move out. Like the snake Mama told Iris about, how it would find some rough place to scrape against to rid itself of the smoke misting its eyes, the tightness that bound it.

I stood up. We had said enough, it was time to go.

"You're off?" Mama shook the colander. "You can bring some beans to Iris."

"I'm not going there. Not until she asks me."

Mama nodded. She lifted out a handful of beans and wrapped them in newspaper. "Take them for Matthew's dinner." She folded the paper carefully. "He's been your work for twenty years, maybe it's time you start thinking about your own."

She touched my hand, and I felt as if I were standing in a green field.

Another Mountain

Jesse, his leg in a cast propped on a bucket, spent the afternoon on the car seat outside the trailer and watched the electric company rig through the scope of his deer rifle. They were putting in poles to bring a power line up to the place. Since his accident, he's been as restless as a chained bear, and I was glad he had that to occupy him, but it gave me the creeps, him aiming the gun at the guys working.

"It's not loaded." He'd opened his hand to show me the shells. "There's Hank coming now."

Hank Heller's pickup turned off the road and started up the track. Bramble, Jesse's bluetick hound, got up from her dust hole beside the steps and stood foursquare watching the truck pull in beside my Mustang. She doesn't like Hank Heller. Hank pulled in fast, then went round to lift an ice chest from the truck bed. He set it on the ground beside Jesse and flipped the lid up. It was packed with beer. He popped a can and reached to help himself from the bag of potato chips I'd brought out for Jesse.

"The bass are turning over in the river," he said.

"Shit," Jesse tapped his beer against the cast, "I'm grounded."

I was damned if I'd sit around listening to them compare fishing stories and went in to collect my keys.

"Drink yourself blind, Hank Heller," I said, "but get your truck out of here without gouging tracks in the field this time."

Jesse looked up sharp. "You leaving?"

"You bet," I started toward the car. "I'm going to Grams's."

Jesse hasn't wanted me out of earshot since he got back from the hospital two weeks ago. He comes to work with me. It's only over the hill to his dad's junked car lot, but the track's rough. I drive it real slow knowing every stone jolts the broken bone. Tom's office is a walled-off corner of the barn with a desk, a phone, and the TV Tom brought from the house for Jesse, who plunks himself in front of the screen while we work. Lord knows how he hears anything with the air compressor and torches going.

Bramble doesn't usually leave Jesse, but she followed me to my Mustang. "You stay," I said and slammed the door. I turned down toward the town road. The guys in the power truck were packing up to quit and waved as I passed. It's a pretty drive over to Grams's across the ridge. When you get to the top, you can see the valley and the next ridge beyond. I always think of the song we sang in Brownies about the bear that went over the mountain to see what he could see. I was glad to be by myself for a bit. Jesse's good company when we're alone, but when he's with his buddies, it's as if I'm not there.

Grams was on the porch glider listening to the evening news from a radio in the kitchen window. After I gave her a hug, she reached back to snap off the radio. I like that about Grams. Jesse and his father keep the TV going all the time; their eyes keep drifting over to the screen when they talk. Drives me crazy.

She had set a row of tomatoes to ripen on the porch rail, and I realized it had been a couple of weeks since I'd visited. Last time I was here, she'd made us a green tomato omelette.

"They're putting in the poles today," I said. "They've got a big rig with a drill."

"They dug the holes by hand when they brought the electric in here." She looked toward the swag of wire looping in from the road. "We had one light in each room; a bare bulb hung from the ceiling. My brother and I squabbled over which of us would pull the string to turn it on."

Grams still has a shelf of old kerosene lamps in the cellar. She likes to keep things. The same linoleum has covered the living room floor since I was a kid. It looks like a rug with borders and flower designs, even has a printed fringe. I used to play there with toy cars using the lines as roads.

"Your mother called," Grams said. "She's coming up tomorrow."

"To check on me?"

"She didn't say."

"Why does she interfere?"

"Your mother's dutiful."

150

Sometimes I think Grams doesn't much like my mother. It's funny, but then I find myself making excuses for Mom.

"She's afraid I won't go back to college."

Grams was turning the green side of the tomatoes toward the light and didn't say anything.

"She meddles in my life and doesn't even know what's going on."

"And you do?"

"Jesse's building me a studio."

"You never wake up wondering how he'll be today?"

A swallow flicked low past the porch, and I felt the small whir of its wing beat. "It's hard with a cast up to his hip," I said.

Grams was silent so long I wondered what my words meant.

"Well, since you're here, you can help me fetch the mason jars from the cellar. I'll be putting up tomatoes by the end of the week. The green beans is ready now."

It was after dark when I got back to the trailer. Hank Heller's truck was still there and a Bronco 4-by I didn't recognize. I turned off the engine and sat behind the wheel watching the place. Shafts of white light from the Coleman lantern lay across the grass; the trailer seemed to bulge with brightness, and voices rolled out the open window. I didn't want to go in. After a bit, someone banged open the door; it could have been Hank, but in the dark it was hard to say.

"Where's that fancy piece of yours?" The voice, aimed outward, startled me with its loudness. Then a spatter of pee stirred the grass.

When he went back in and closed the door, I started the motor, and without turning on the lights, drove up the track to the top of the ridge. I could see the roof of the trailer and the parked trucks. Everything was still except for an occasional burst of laughter and a whippoorwill sounding off in the pasture below. Cool air moved through the pines carrying the smell of pitch.

Tomorrow I'd have plenty to clean up: beer cans, cigarettes, and joint butts. We don't yet have water to hose down the grass below the steps, and my mother has a nose like a beagle. When she came by a couple of weeks ago, it was clear she hated the place. She'd stood in front of the trailer, her dress buttoned up to the neck and every hair in order, almost quivering with disapproval. She hadn't taken to Jesse either. Grams said something about my being pleased to shock her. I didn't much want to remember that conversation; it made me feel mean. Mom spoke about choices, but she didn't say how she chose. She was crying when she left, and I didn't say good-bye.

Last week, Jesse's father came over to grill steaks, and after a couple of beers, began talking about Mom. They had gone to school together, and I think he fancied her. She was different from other girls, he said; she wanted to be a vet, to take care of animals. I hadn't known that. Dad had asthma, and we weren't allowed to have pets. I didn't know she had to give up animals, although I might have guessed. The time Mark brought a puppy home, she stood up to Dad and said he could keep it in the garage, but after a week of Dad hacking and coughing, she gave up. I wondered if I would have liked Mom when she was a girl. I hadn't thought about liking her before.

The trailer door slammed. If you don't watch it, it hits against the siding. Someone crossed to the Bronco and reached in the window, for a bottle probably; they'd be into the hard stuff. Had Jesse noticed I wasn't home? Yesterday, he was sore when I was twenty minutes late coming back from the A & P, but by now he'd be half crocked and wouldn't care.

I got out and leaned against the car. The stars were bright, and Scorpio rose over the valley to the south. A guy in my English class had showed me the constellations. We used to climb out on the dorm roof and sit with our backs against the slope. He pointed out Orion the Hunter, the Water Bearer, Pegasus. Lovely names. I wanted to take astronomy.

I felt a small jolt remembering school. I hadn't thought about it much since I'd met Jesse. That was in May, when Grams told me to go to Tom's junkyard to find another muffler and tailpipe for my Mustang. I borrowed Tom's torch, and he watched me take off the muffler, then offered me a job on the spot.

In college I signed up for welding, but it turned out to be metal sculpture. The instructor taught us about mass and balance and how, when objects are put together, they respond to each other. It was great; I began to look around at things in a new way. I made a goat for Grams out of bits of an old stove I found. The work I do for Tom is mostly taking apart, but I've learned a lot from him. He knows metal, talks about weight and temper. Welding is what he did in the navy.

A couple of weeks ago, I had this idea for a piece with bears—Ursa Major and Ursa Minor. I wanted to show them in space, using wire and maybe bits of glass, like broken Coke bottles. But stars aren't on the same plane; I needed to know about that. It's not just shape, but how the figures fit together. What's their story? Are they a mother and she cub? I looked for a book on astronomy in the town library, but they only had an encyclopedia and a kid's book on stars. The librarian said to go to the community college, but Jesse broke his leg, and I haven't been back to it.

I could make out the tail of the bear where it dropped behind the trees and Polaris above it. Nice to know one star stays in the same place. I heard the trailer door bang open, and Hank stumbled out toward his truck. He yelled something over his shoulder like he was sore, then climbed in and started the engine. The truck jerked back then pitched forward; the headlights caught in the tall grass as he careened down toward the town road. A while later, two guys came out to the Bronco. They stood around a bit, maybe looking for keys or arguing about who would drive, until one went round to the far side. I watched their taillights buck down the hill.

I got in the car without starting it and let it roll down the track to pull into the space beside Jesse's pickup. I left the keys in the ignition. The trailer door was open, and Bramble came out to greet me. Jesse lay spread across the bed on his back and aligned alongside his cast was his rifle. I couldn't tell if he was awake or not, then remembered what Grams had asked me. I didn't know how he would be.

I called his name from the doorway, but he didn't stir. When I said it again and he still didn't answer, I crossed to the bed. His eyes were closed; he breathed heavily and his right hand lay on the butt of his gun. I pulled it toward me firm and quick the way you do with jackstraws. His hand flapped on the bed, but he didn't wake. Out on the steps, I clicked open the chamber and spilled the shells into my hand. I took the rifle to the car and set it on the back seat, the shells I dropped into my jeans pocket.

Inside the trailer, the light was growing dim. Either the Coleman was running out of gas, or it needed to be pumped up. I didn't much want to go back in; the place was a mess and reeked of smoke. My room at Grams's was always there waiting. As I went to check the lamp, my foot hit an empty can, spinning it across the floor. Jesse raised his head.

"Shit," he said. "I had you smashed up on the road."

He didn't sound thick when he spoke, and he smiled slow as if to welcome me in beside him. But then his head dropped back, and he was asleep again. I pumped up the lamp and pulled out a plastic bag to collect the empties. This was what I had to do. It was too easy to leave; Grams has always been my fallback. The day Mom came by and got so het up, I went straight to Grams. She told me to go do my work, but didn't say what it was.

The cans I chucked into the bag were squashed or twisted. At the Log Cabin, Hank would take one between his thumb and finger and squeeze it flat. Then Jesse would have to do the same. He gets that way. I swept broken pretzels from the floor and washed out the glasses and a plate someone had used as an ashtray. I threw the soapy water below the steps and sponged out the sink. We have to be careful about water. Jesse set up a barrel to collect rain from the trailer roof, and we bring a five-gallon jug from his dad's every day.

Jesse thinks of ways to fix up the place, like the real leather seats he took out of a T-bird and the tool shed he made from a couple of truck hoods. He worked a swap with a friend who runs a Porta-John business—a chassis repair job in exchange for a couple of months service.

The lamp started to dim again, and the hiss drew in. I undressed in the last wavering light before it flicked out. As I lay down beside Jesse, he reached his hand across my belly.

I woke early. In spite of my cleaning, the place felt dingy, the air sour. I made coffee on the gas ring and carried a mug outside. The ridge keeps the trailer in shadow a good hour after sunrise, and the car seat was still wet with dew, so I walked up the track to where the sun hit an outcrop overlooking the valley. Mom would come today. I should pick wildflowers and set them in a jar; she'd like that. The trailer hadn't improved much since she was here last. We'd been all set to paint the place before Jesse broke his leg. And I hadn't done any work on my sculpture. For a moment, my mind flashed to the bears, but I pushed the thought away. I had other things to do.

When I got back, Jesse was sitting on the bed.

"Where the hell were you?"

"Looking at the morning."

"Where's the aspirin?"

I started toward the cabinet, but an image of my mother made me stop. If my father said there was no sugar bowl on the table, she'd leap up and fetch it for him.

"In the cabinet," I said and poured myself another coffee.

Jesse lay still and watched me from the bed.

"Grams says Mom's coming today." I pulled my welding gloves from the shelf. If I don't keep them here, they disappear from the shop. "I got to go," I said. "Tom has a dealer coming this afternoon, and the parts aren't ready."

I thought he'd want to drive over with me, but he sat without moving. In the doorway, I turned and said, "Coffee's on the stove."

He didn't even nod.

Grams's question flicked across my mind again. How would he be? When I opened the car door and saw the rifle on the back seat, I felt a ping in my belly. I set the gun on the floor and covered it with a couple of sheets of newspaper.

Tom and I worked all morning cleaning up universal joints we'd taken off a couple of Ford trucks. At noon, I drove back over the ridge. The power company truck had left, and Jesse wasn't on the seat outside the trailer. The door was open, and as I walked in, I smelled acrylic paint. The place seemed brighter; the bed and dresser had been pulled out, and the wall was painted a clean white. I didn't see Jesse right away, he was sitting on a milk crate with his cast stretched out, working on the baseboards.

"Hey, it looks great."

"We can move the stuff back in a half an hour," he said. "It'll be tacky, but it's OK if we're careful."

The sun was behind him, and I couldn't see his face, but he held the brush out from himself like a torch.

"How did you manage?" I said.

"When does she get here?"

"She'll stop at Grams's first. Tom said I could take the afternoon off."

I laid slices of bread on the counter and pulled one of Grams's tomatoes out of the cooler.

"What's she coming for?"

"Probably to ask if she should send in the check for next semester."

I heard Jesse slide the bucket along the floor, but I didn't look at him.

"What are you going to tell her?"

"I don't know." The knife was dull, and I had to use the tip to break the tomato's skin. "Want mayo?"

"We've got a couple of hours yet. I can finish the back wall."

Before I put the sandwiches on plates, I cut each one diagonally to make two triangles.

"Let's eat first."

"I'm not hungry."

"You're hungover."

"Shit. You'll be saying that three times a week for the rest of our lives."

I started to say that's not so, but stopped and stared at the three-sided sandwiches. That was how my mother always cut them. I was doing what she did. Was I choosing the same way she had? Grams said to find my work. Was taking care of Jesse what I had to do? That's how it would be: Jesse staggering back in from the Log Cabin, me getting sore, then us doing good things for each other for a few days but always walking the edge, trying to forget it was the edge, that it would happen again.

"The rest of our lives," is what I said.

Jesse must have heard something in my voice. He lifted his head, his hand holding the brush. "You're leaving, aren't you?"

"I don't know."

"But you're going to; you're going to leave."

I wasn't sure if he was telling me or threatening me, and I didn't know until that instant, he was right.

"Yes," I said.

He reached out and pulled his crutches to him. "Then leave. Leave now."

"You mean that?"

"You're damned right."

One look at his face, and I knew he meant it. I dragged my suitcase out of the closet, swept my clothes off the rod and dropped them into the case, then scooped everything from the top drawer of the dresser. Jesse pulled himself up with his good leg, set his hands on the grips of his crutches and swung fast to the bed. With one of the crutches he lifted the quilt.

"Where is it?"

The latch of the case was stiff; I leaned to close it. "In my car." I stood up.

"I want it."

"You'll get it."

I carried the suitcase out and opened the hatch. I went to the shed for my welding gear; grabbed the helmet, gloves, and steel toolbox; and set them beside my suitcase. The hose and pressure gauges were fastened to the tank, and I took a wrench to undo them.

Jesse came through the door of the trailer with Bramble beside him and paused on the stoop. He rarely makes an awkward move, but to maneuver the steps, he bent forward and dropped down with a jerk. I finished unscrewing the hoses, bundled them together, and slammed the hatch closed. He was on the bottom step. I reached to the backseat for the gun and walked to the far side of his pickup and set it on the cab floor.

Jesse moved fast across the clay ground. His shoulders took the weight of his body; his good leg reached out carrying him forward in a neat arc. His face was as empty as if he saw nothing, as if crossing the yard took all his attention.

"It's in the cab," I said. "Good-bye, Jesse."

The Mustang caught on the first turn of the key. Jesse was already level with the front fender of the pickup. The shells in my pocket bulged on my thigh, but I knew he kept a box in the glove compartment.

As I backed the car out, I caught a glimpse of him reaching into the cab. The smell of pitch lay sweet on the air, and the tires made a familiar sound on the gravel. The grass was flattened where the electric company truck had parked this morning. I thought of Jesse's blue eye pressed against the scope, crosshairs in a circle of light, his thumb closing focus on the moving car. Goldenrod whipped past, a pair of doves broke from the field. As I turned onto the township road, I could see the trailer with pines behind it, the blue truck, and Jesse. The sun gleamed on something; I couldn't tell if it was the gun or his crutch. Then I saw him outlined against the pines, his hands on Bramble's head.

I didn't trust Jesse; I knew that now. Was this how I made a decision—letting events take over, stumbling into action? Was this what my mother did?

The road sloped steeply up the ridge, and at the top I pulled over to the side where I could see the country beyond. That was it: the valley, another mountain, another valley. Pasture, barns, woodlots. Grams's house lay just below the next ridge; I could make out the barn roof. She and Mom would be sitting on the porch with cups of coffee. I had to deal with them first, then I could go for the things I didn't know—the story of the bears, Ursa Major, Ursa Minor. It was a start.

About the Author

Ann B. Knox, returning to the U.S. after living overseas for twenty years, received her M.A. in education, and taught elementary and junior high school for nine years. When her children grew up and her husband left, she moved to a cabin on the edge of the Appalachians for solitude. As she approached sixty, she received an M.F.A. in writing from Warren Wilson College. She is currently the editor of *Antietam Review* and teaches fiction at the Writers' Center in Washington, D.C. Ms. Knox lives in Hancock, Maryland.

Papier-Mache Press

At Papier-Mache Press, it is our goal to identify and successfully present important social issues through enduring works of beauty, grace, and strength. Through our work we hope to encourage empathy and respect among diverse communities, creating a bridge of understanding between the mainstream audience and those who might not otherwise be heard.

We appreciate you, our customer, and strive to earn your continued support. We also value the role of the bookseller in achieving our goals. We are especially grateful to the many independent booksellers whose presence ensures a continuing diversity of opinion, information, and literature in our communities. We encourage you to support these bookstores with your patronage.

We publish many fine books about women's experiences. We also produce lovely posters and T-shirts that complement our anthologies. Please ask your local bookstore which Papier-Mache items they carry. To receive our complete catalog, please send your request to Papier-Mache Press, 135 Aviation Way, #14, Watsonville, CA 95076, or call our toll-free number, 800-927-5913.